Shotgun Ridge was foun [barcode obscures text]
Addie Malone, a woman [barcode obscures text]
on five thieves and strong enough to tame the land around her. Now the town needed more women like Addie to rustle up its bachelors, make roots and keep Shotgun Ridge thriving. Four matchmaking old men were determined to help nature take its course, and this time they had their sights set on Ethan Callahan, the town playboy.

***

Ethan lowered his head, stopped just bare inches from Dora's lips, kept his gaze on hers. "Tell me something, legs. Where did you learn those bidding skills you displayed earlier?"

Dora tilted her chin, brushed her lower body against his deliberately. "At my daddy's church."

Her breath was warm against his lips, firing his fantasies. "Your daddy's— You're a preacher's daughter?"

"Is that a problem?"

The little wench was doing her best not to laugh at him. "You're darned right it's a problem. I nearly seduced you right here in the bedroom."

"Oh, believe me, cowboy. You were a *long* way from seducing *me*."

Dear Reader,

Welcome to another joy-filled month of heart, home and happiness from Harlequin American Romance! We're pleased to bring you four new stories filled with people you'll always remember and romance you'll never forget.

We've got more excitement for you this month as MAITLAND MATERNITY continues with Jacqueline Diamond's *I Do! I Do!* An elusive bachelor marries a lovely nurse for the sake of his twin nieces— will love turn their house into a home? Watch for twelve new books in this heartwarming series, starting next month from Harlequin Books!

How does a proper preacher's daughter tame the wildest man in the county? With a little help from a few Montana matchmakers determined to repopulate their town! Sparks are sure to fly in *The Playboy's Own Miss Prim*, the latest BACHELORS OF SHOTGUN RIDGE story by Mindy Neff!

An expectant mother, blinded from an accident, learns that the heart recognizes what the eye cannot see in Lisa Bingham's touching novel *Man Behind the Voice*. And when a little boy refuses to leave his ranch home, his mother must make a deal with the brooding, sexy new owner. Don't miss Carol Grace's delightful *Family Tree*.

Spice up your summer days with the best of Harlequin American Romance!

Warm wishes,

Melissa Jeglinski
Associate Senior Editor

The Playboy's Own Miss Prim

MINDY NEFF

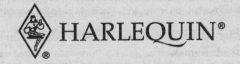

HARLEQUIN®

TORONTO • NEW YORK • LONDON
AMSTERDAM • PARIS • SYDNEY • HAMBURG
STOCKHOLM • ATHENS • TOKYO • MILAN • MADRID
PRAGUE • WARSAW • BUDAPEST • AUCKLAND

To Cherie:

For brainstorming about cowboys and sexy guys—and for the friendship. Thanks, girlfriend.

A billion hugs!

ISBN 0-373-16834-9

THE PLAYBOY'S OWN MISS PRIM

Copyright © 2000 by Melinda Neff.

This edition published by arrangement with Harlequin Books S.A.

® and TM are trademarks of the publisher. Trademarks indicated with ® are registered in the United States Patent and Trademark Office, the Canadian Trade Marks Office and in other countries.

Visit us at www.eHarlequin.com

Printed in U.S.A.

ABOUT THE AUTHOR

Originally from Louisiana, Mindy Neff settled in Southern California, where she married a really romantic guy and raised five great kids. Family, friends, writing and reading are her passions. When not writing, Mindy's ideal getaway is a good book, hot sunshine and a chair at the river's edge with water lapping at her toes.

Mindy loves to hear from readers and can be reached at P.O. Box 2704-262, Huntington Beach, CA 92647.

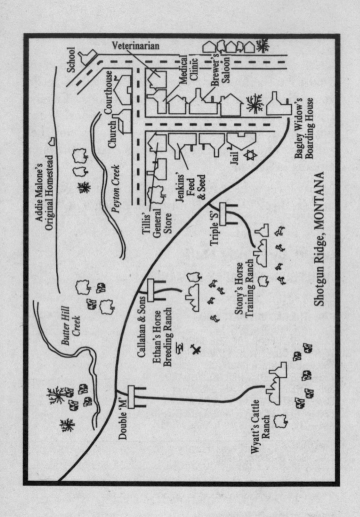

Shotgun Ridge, MONTANA

School

Veterinarian

Medical Clinic

Brewer's Saloon

Courthouse

Church

Addie Malone's Original Homestead

Peyton Creek

Bagley Widow's Boarding House

Jail

Jenkins' Feed & Seed

Tillis' General Store

Triple "S"

Butter Hill Creek

Callahan & Sons Ethan's Horse Breeding Ranch

Stony's Horse Training Ranch

Double "M"

Wyatt's Cattle Ranch

Prologue

*Well, it pains me to say that Vanessa—God rest
her sweet soul—is not real sure about this next
plan me and the boys have hatched.*

Ozzie Peyton glanced lovingly at the oil painting of
his beloved Vanessa that hung over the stone fire-
place. For a moment the flicker of lamplight danced
over the delicate blush of her face, and Ozzie could
have sworn he saw her cherry lips curve. He gave a
smile and turned his attention back to his journal writing. Folks didn't realize he consulted Vanessa about
everything he did. They just wouldn't understand.

He licked the end of his medium-tip, black ink pen.

*Me and Lloyd and Henry and Vern read a news-
paper piece on an outfit out in Los Angeles, California, that held a fancy biddin' auction where
the goods was a handsome, interesting date for
the night. This shindig was for a charity cause—
and that got us to thinkin' we ought to do something like that right here in town. Besides, Ver-*

non pointed out that Shotgun Ridge was as good a cause for charity as anything. After all, we're dying here. In a town with mostly men and hardly any young women, everybody agrees that we're definitely ailing.

I tell you what, though, we've got a pretty darn good start—on getting us some women, that is. Was a little touch-and-go there for a while, but Wyatt Malone is happier than a cow in clover over his new family.

And that's what our cause is all about. Women and babies and families. Vanessa warned me to take it slow, and that's how come we've waited such a spell to make our next move. (That and the fact that none of us wanted to admit we didn't know the first thing about no bachelor auctions.) And the more we got into it, the more nervous we got—especially Lloyd, but I think that was on account of his Mrs. (Iris) jawing at him. She tends to do that a lot, but Lloyd don't seem to mind.

Anyhow, we got to worrying that we might have jumped into a situation where we couldn't at least halfway guarantee the outcome—and I gotta say, controlling the outcome of most anything is a big thing with me. A fault, I'm told, but there it is. Take me as I am.

Vanessa, good woman that she is, never said a cross word or an "I told you so." That's because she always had such faith in me, and that's something that makes a man feel about ten feet tall.

But I'm digressing here. Me and the boys got a mite worried over this here bachelor auction we had planned—and I mean we had it planned. Yessiree, right down to the catered dinner and the requiring of fancy duds. Just so happens there's this new little gal in town who does the best cooking and catering…but more on her at another time.

Right now me and the boys are concentrating on Ethan Callahan. A ladies' man if there ever was one. And a fine catch. But he's so busy lovin' 'em all, he's missing out on the joy of lovin' just the one.

But like I was sayin', this auction shindig threatened to get totally out of our hands, and I'm kind of liking the idea of being able to nudge here and there, to choose just the right match for just the right fellow. 'Cept my mind don't work in a bunch of directions at once, and I like to concentrate on one thing at a time—a hard thing to do when you can't control who's biddin' on who. Me and the boys had a scuffle or two over it—no punches thrown, mind you, but a few verbal barbs. And then, right about the time I was all set to scrap the whole idea, the details fell into place like a lasso over a calf's neck. 'Course we all should have known and trusted that the good Lord does his best work in mysterious ways. (Vanessa had to remind me of that, and I did appreciate it.)

And wouldn't ya just know it, the perfect little

filly has turned up....

Never mind Vernon's comment about saints and sinners and babies...I'm *not* questioning the Man Upstairs on this one!

Chapter One

Ethan Callahan tugged at the collar of his tuxedo shirt. He owned two of these penguin suits, was comfortable in them, but he'd just as soon be wearing his jeans and hat.

He couldn't believe he'd actually let the old folks railroad him into this ridiculous bachelor auction. A black-tie affair at Brewer's Saloon, of all places. Owned by Lloyd and Iris Brewer, it was down-home cooking, jukebox tunes and the gathering place for friends and visitors to the town of Shotgun Ridge, Montana.

"Well, now. You look right dapper," Ozzie Peyton said. "You bet."

"I feel like an idiot." He half glared at the three old fellas who considered themselves the town matchmakers. The fourth was out in the main room of the saloon on a makeshift stage gleefully emceeing the auction.

They'd gotten it into their heads that the town needed women and babies. And their latest scheme to accomplish that goal was this bachelor auction.

Well they could just turn their sights on someone else. Ethan had no intention of getting married and having babies. He liked his life just the way it was, thank you very much.

He'd agreed to be auctioned off. One date. One night. Fairly harmless if a man stayed on his toes. And if he were to be totally honest, he'd have to admit that it could be fun. He loved women, considered himself a connoisseur of sorts, so a date with one wouldn't be a hardship at all.

But he wasn't going to admit that to any one of the four old matchmakers. They were too full of themselves as it was.

"I don't know why you won't just let me write you a check. You know I can afford to give you a lot more than you'll make on this fiasco."

"Oh, stop your fussin' and your braggin'," Ozzie admonished, giving a tug to Ethan's bow tie.

Ethan smothered a grin as he looked down at Shotgun Ridge's mayor. Seventy-something, Ozzie was still sharp as a tack, with steel-gray hair and piercing blue eyes. The man meddled, but he was genuinely goodhearted. And he was acting kind of strange, fidgety.

"She should've been here." Ozzie muttered to himself.

"Who?"

The old man's hand stilled, then he brushed at a nonexistent speck of lint on Ethan's tuxedo jacket, his vivid eyes wide with false innocence. "No one, uh, I mean Iris should have been back here by now to get you."

That was a blatant lie, and Ethan started to get a bad feeling. He remembered what the four meddlers had done to his neighbor and friend, Wyatt Malone. Presented him with a mail-order bride. Hannah and her son, Ian, were exactly what Wyatt had needed, and Ethan had even found himself aiding and abetting. *Matchmaking,* he thought with a shudder—but he wasn't going to be caught in the same trap. "What are you up to, Ozzie?"

"I've never known you to be dense, son." Ozzie gave him a pitying look. "We're up to a bachelor auction, that's what. You bet. And I just imagine a fair amount of these ladies will want to stay right here in Shotgun Ridge. A fine class they are, too. They got money to buy a date, they're likely high quality, and if they take it in their heads to migrate here to our fine town, well that's just a bonus."

"Ozzie Peyton, you're sounding like a snob."

"I am not." He looked appalled. "Rich or poor, an executive or a…a church girl, they'll be welcome. Now put on that lady-killer smile and get ready to go on the stage. I'll just run on out and see how things are going. You bet."

Ozzie rushed out, and Ethan felt nerves crowd in. For crying out loud, it was only a little acting, a stroll down a raised plywood stage, a couple of turns. He was master of his own destiny, he reminded himself, a sophisticated man. He'd once dated a press secretary at the White House and dined with the president. He could handle five minutes on a stage.

As much as he pretended to gripe, there wasn't

anything he wouldn't do for Ozzie Peyton or this town. He owed them.

But when he got home, he was going to kill his two brothers for hightailing it out of town and abandoning him this way.

"Okay, Ethan, you're on." Vern and Henry all but shoved him through the swinging saloon doors and onto the stage.

"Ladies and gentlemen, we've got a treat for sure," Lloyd extolled, his voice booming through the microphone. "This here's our major beef—not to disparage any of our other fine bachelors, mind you."

Major beef? For the love of God, Ethan felt his face heat with the flush of embarrassment.

"Our next and final bachelor up for bid is Ethan Callahan. A fine catch, I'm telling you. A renown horse breeder residing right here in Shotgun Ridge. If it's a fancy five-star dinner in a swanky city you've a hankering for, or a hike through Yellowstone, this man has the means to make your dreams come true. He'll fly you there in his own personal airplane or squire you in one of his flashy cars—though I'm sure there's a sin somewhere in owning more than one pleasure vehicle," Lloyd added dryly.

Hoots and hollers ensued, and it was just the thing to relax Ethan. He was extremely proud of every one of his toys, from the 'Vette to the chopper. And if Lloyd teasingly hinted that it was gluttony to own three cars as well as all the other stuff, so be it. Pastor Lucas would just have to pray harder over Ethan's soul.

Because Ethan was a man who loved to have fun.

And from the sound and enthusiasm of this crowd, they were definitely festive and out for a good time.

Okay, he thought, grinning and winking at a brunette in gold sequins. *I can get into this.*

Unbuttoning his tuxedo jacket, he slid a hand in one pocket of his trousers and poured on the charm, working the crowd of women who were raising their hands faster than Lloyd could ask for a bid or raise the amount.

His grin widened, and he scanned the room. He had to hand it to the old guys. They knew how to pack a room and they threw a heck of a party. The place was filled with glittering, sweet-smelling ladies. At this rate the town balance was likely to tip in the opposite direction—too many women and not enough cowboys. He kind of liked the sound of that.

Competitive spirit and ego reared up as he worked the room with his eyes, enticing women to up their bids. If he had to be a part of this crazy plan, he might as well turn it into a challenge, make sure he commanded a higher price than his neighbors or employees.

His gaze swept past the door, then slammed back, causing him to stop his performance mid-stride.

Oh, man, he thought when his brain finally kicked back in gear. *Here comes trouble in a tight pair of jeans.*

As though he'd spoken the thought aloud, her gaze honed in on his, held.

And for an instant Ethan forgot to draw a breath.

She was a dynamite package, self-assured, holding

his stare when most women would have coyly looked away. That alone intrigued him…and turned him on.

He raised a brow. An invitation.

She appeared to struggle with a reluctant smile, then shifted her attention, only pausing for a bare instant as she noted the dressy attire in the rest of the room versus her casual sweater and jeans. With a nearly imperceptible shrug, she gave her head a gentle shake, flicked her honey-blond hair off her shoulders and strolled into the room as though she wore a sexy floor-length silk gown and diamonds. With a smile she let Ozzie direct her to an empty seat. Right up front.

Mmm, yes indeed, Ethan thought, following her progress with his eyes, his gaze riveted on the sassy sway of her hips in those skintight jeans. *Mighty fine.*

Suddenly the evening took on a new energy.

But he was falling down on his performance. He was supposed to flirt with *all* the women. Even though he'd already set his sights on just the one.

He smiled at a man in the audience who'd obviously been intrigued by the blonde's entrance, too, and the man smiled back. A guy-to-guy communication, Ethan thought, then missed a step when the young man raised his hand.

Surely not.

A slight frown tugged at his brows. Lloyd accepted the bid, then another right on its heels—from a woman, thank God. And then…

Shocked, Ethan watched the guy raise his hand again. He nearly stumbled, actually stopped moving for a full five seconds and gawked. Then he jerked his gaze away. Was he encouraging the guy? *A guy!*

The dish in jeans gave a nod of her head, and Lloyd acknowledged it. Ethan started to breathe easier, and told himself he would *not* look back at the male bidder. But he did. And the man's hand was up again.

Genuine panic set in.

My God, the bid was already up to five thousand dollars!

Lloyd was apparently having trouble with his voice and his reflexes, because he was extremely slow to notice when the blonde put her hand up again. He was too busy staring, flabbergasted, at the man who was bidding.

Ethan was beginning to think he'd have to totally embarrass himself and point out the woman who was discreetly attempting to top the bid. He felt a bit like a dog running in circles trying to get his master's attention, and he nearly shouted out the acknowledgment himself. But Lloyd found his stride once more.

And darn it all, studly tuxedo man raised his hand again.

Ethan's brows slammed down. My God, *nothing* had prepared him for this.

The room went silent.

"Six thousand going once..." Lloyd called, a nervous quaver to his voice.

No one made a move.

Ethan's gaze whipped to the blonde. She was actually smirking. Okay, fine. Six thousand dollars was a staggering amount of money to most people. He'd pay it himself, he tried to tell her with his eyes.

"Six thousand going twice…"

"Please!" He formed the word silently with his mouth.

Dora Watkins struggled valiantly with her grin. She'd never seen a sexy cowboy so flustered. And she'd heard enough about playboy Ethan Callahan to know that wasn't a characteristic state for him.

When her father had told her to meet up with Ozzie Peyton at Brewer's Saloon for an introduction to the wealthy Shotgun Ridge cowboy, she'd had no idea it would be in the middle of a bachelor auction. But Dora was known to think on her feet and take most anything in stride.

And at the moment she was enjoying herself immensely.

Ozzie elbowed her. "Well, come on, girl. Put the boy out of his misery. You come here for him. Might as well be able to call the shots. You buy him, he's gotta give you all his attention. And I'll personally see to it he pays for the date himself."

"You know that's not strictly necessary. I've got gobs of money." Her grandfather was Texas oilman, Quentin Watkins. Her trust fund alone was more than most people saw in a lifetime—somewhat to the dismay of her conservative parents. "But I didn't come here for him. Katie did."

"Same thing." He winked. "You bet."

Darned if she didn't like this old man. He was intent on matchmaking and being obvious about it. She'd perused the program when she'd sat down, read the captioned advertisement they'd obviously run in the city papers:

Come to Shotgun Ridge's Cowboy Bachelor Auction. Have a Date That'll Likely End in a Marriage Proposal.

Dora wondered if any of the cowboys had seen that little tidbit on the program.

But Dora wasn't here for matchmaking or marriage. She only wanted one thing from Ethan Callahan.

Custody of Katie for herself.

But before she could ask for that, she had to uphold her promise to Amanda. She had to give Ethan a chance to know his daughter.

One month, she told herself. Then he would be begging her to take the baby and leave him to his playboy cowboy ways.

She looked back at the plea in Ethan's sexy blue eyes, saw a trickle of sweat make its way down his temple.

Her smile widened. She didn't in any way think this man could be tamed, but she liked the power she held just now.

"Going—"

"Seven thousand." She said it aloud, calmly, and for an instant not a soul in the room moved.

Ethan whipped around and glared at the male bidder. It was a fierce look that would have had the meanest grizzly apologizing for daring to show his face.

The man shrugged and shook his head, ceding to Dora's thousand-dollar raise.

"Sold!" Lloyd shouted and banged a gavel on the dais.

Ethan's shoulders visibly relaxed. His gaze when he turned it back to her was tender and filled with emotion. It was a look that stole her breath and made her knees tremble.

"Thank you." Again the words were silently formed.

She inclined her head and got up, needing a breath of air.

She had to collect herself before she confronted the man who had every legal right to the child she desperately wanted.

ETHAN STEPPED DOWN off the stage more relieved than he cared to admit. What had started out as fun had nearly turned to panic. Man, that kind of thing had never happened to him before.

As he made his way through the crowd of women, pausing to speak to a few, he couldn't stop thinking about the little blonde who'd bought a date with him. She'd been so calm, so self-assured, never even batted an eye at the amount.

With her smile wide and her eyes locked to his, she'd been toying with him. Now that he was able to relax, he could appreciate her verve, her sass. She was a woman he could spend a while on. Instinctively he knew he wouldn't be bored.

Nodding to several of his neighbors and skirting a cluster of women getting to know their cowboy dates, Ethan looked up and came face-to-face with the young man who'd nearly shaken his cool.

He reached up to tug his hat before he realized he wasn't wearing one.

The young man extended his hand, and Ethan stared at it as though it was a diamondback rattler. This was ridiculous, he knew.

He accepted the handshake, gripping harder than usual just to make himself feel better, to establish his position in case there was any question as to what his preference was.

"Tyler Redding," the man said. "I apologize for making you uncomfortable."

In a strictly objective sense, Ethan allowed that Tyler Redding was a decent-looking guy. His jet-black tuxedo spoke of wealth, and his shoulders beneath the jacket were broad on a body kept in good shape.

"I have to ask..." He didn't quite know how to form the words. "Did I do something that gave you the impression I was...that we could...?" He couldn't finish. And now that he'd bumbled through the vague question, he wasn't sure he wanted an answer. His masculinity was smarting.

Tyler shouted with laughter, and Ethan looked around to see if the outburst had drawn attention. It had. Great.

"That's one of the reasons I stopped you," Tyler said. "I figured you had the wrong idea and thought I'd better straighten things out. I was trying to get a date for my sister. She's too shy to bid on her own."

"Oh." *Thank God.* Given that the room was filled with women, he could be forgiven for not noticing a shy one next to Tyler. "Well, then. No harm, no foul."

Tyler shoved his hands in his pockets and turned. "Enjoy your date. And it better be something really good for that price."

Ethan hadn't even thought of that. It was only his bad luck that one of his mares had gone into premature labor. Otherwise he'd have been out of town with his brothers and would have escaped this fiasco.

Instead, he'd been wide open for Ozzie and company to corner him, to shame him into doing his duty for the town.

He remembered coming here as a wary eight-year-old. Remembered this town—headed by Ozzie and Vanessa Peyton—rallying around Fred Callahan in his quest to adopt three messed-up boys who didn't know the first thing about love and family. But with the help of all the citizens in Shotgun Ridge, Fred Callahan had taught Ethan and his brothers just that.

Ethan owed the town.

But was he supposed to parade himself, nearly get bought by a man *and* organize the date?

Recalling the small, spunky woman, his body sent several highly appealing ideas to his brain.

He moved through the swinging saloon doors into the room that was normally set up for pool tables, dancing and—most recently—a cordoned-off section for cigar smoking.

Ozzie, Lloyd, Henry and Vern were lined up like crows watching a cornfield. Ethan felt his heart soften. Their intentions were good. But as much as he was attracted to the sexy blonde who'd "bought" him, could picture himself having more than one date with her, getting to know her, he wasn't about to settle into marriage.

"So where's my date?" he asked.

"Right here," came a soft voice.

He turned slowly. She was a tiny woman with a presence and assurance that made her appear taller, and a whisky voice that grabbed a man's attention and held him in thrall.

And in her arms, she held a cute baby in a frilly pink dress.

He turned up the wattage of his smile. So she had a kid. No problem. The town was full of willing baby-sitters. "Thanks for bailing me out, darlin'. I gotta tell you, you're more my idea of a fine date than that fella was."

"Oh, I'm not your date...*darlin'.* I bought you for *her.*" She inclined her head toward the baby, who watched him with curious eyes, her little mouth wrapped around a thumb.

"Ethan Callahan, meet your daughter, Kathryn Lynn Callahan."

Chapter Two

Ethan was so stunned it was a moment before her words actually registered. His *daughter?*

He held up his hands, backed away. "I've never seen you before in my life!" My God, had the whole world gone mad tonight?

She shook her head, glanced at the avid audience they had. "Perhaps we could discuss this somewhere more private?"

"Darlin', I promise you, there's nothing to discuss."

"Suit yourself. I've got no problem with telling the whole town about your indiscretions."

Ethan swore and carefully gripped her by the arm that wasn't supporting the baby, almost surprised he could be gentle when his insides were roiling. But Fred Callahan—even though he'd been a bachelor all his life—had taught Ethan and his brothers that woman were to be revered, respected and protected at all costs. No exceptions.

Turning her, he slipped his arm around her waist,

felt her stiffen. He ignored the reaction and steered her outside.

Once they were away from prying eyes and ears, he dropped his arm and turned to face her.

"I'm not sure what game you're playing here, but you've picked the wrong man. I repeat. I've never seen you before in my life, and believe me, sugar, I'd remember. And before you tell me some crazy lie about being too drunk to recall, I'll head you off right now and tell you that's not a possibility." He undid his bow tie with a jerk and snatched open the top button of his shirt.

"Do you always accuse before you know the facts?"

"Depends." His gaze rested on the baby girl who still watched him so closely, her thumb stuck in her mouth. He wasn't a good judge of age, but if he had to guess, he'd estimate a year or younger. He looked back at the woman. "What's your name?"

"Dora Watkins."

He pounced. "See, there? You automatically told me. That's as good as admitting that we've never met."

"Of course. I never said we had."

Her tone was reasonable, soothing, calm. Any minute now he was going to wake up from this crazy nightmare. "But you introduced this child as my daughter."

"And so she is."

"Now hold on a minute—"

"I'm not Katie's mother."

The very softness of her voice, the hint of anguish,

had him looking close. Paying attention. This shed a whole new, scary light on the subject.

Not the mother? Katie was his daughter? Ethan wasn't a saint by any stretch of the imagination, but he prided himself on being careful, of protecting a woman if their relationship became intimate.

"Maybe it's the shock," he said at last, "or this whole crazy auction thing, but I'm having trouble keeping up."

"Do you remember a fishing trip on the Madison?"

"I fish there every…Amanda," he said, an image gelling, touching a soft place in his heart. Almost two years ago.

"Yes. Amanda. She was my best friend."

"Was?"

"She's gone—a tourist who'd had too much alcohol and not enough brains to stay out from behind the wheel of a car."

"I'm sorry." And he was. He'd thought of Amanda over the past two years—and he hadn't even known her last name. He'd gone to Madison for fishing, not sex. Then over a drink at the local pub, he'd met Amanda. And although he hadn't been prepared, she'd been sad and insistent, a combination Ethan couldn't refuse.

With his heart slamming against his ribs like the hooves on a high-strung stallion, he looked down at the baby, swallowed. "Are you sure?" His wealth made him a target, and he had to be careful.

"I'm sure. Your name's on the birth certificate."

"Anybody can pick a name out of a hat and put it

on a birth certificate.'' But something in Dora's lake blue eyes made his gut twist in panic, convinced him that wasn't the case. Pain was there, a raw lick of flame that nearly shouted. As though she loved this baby the way a devoted mother would. That in itself suggested this was no game.

"Katie is your daughter, Ethan. I was with Amanda before, during and after her pregnancy, every step of the way until now. And you mentioned her name before I did.'' She ran a protective hand over the little girl's small shoulder.

A child. He had a child. He didn't know what to think, how to feel, how to react. His lifestyle wasn't one that would easily accommodate children. He hadn't planned on having any. But he couldn't— *wouldn't*—turn his back on responsibility. The enormity of the realization nearly brought him to his knees.

Tentatively he reached out, almost afraid to touch.

The baby's bottom lip poked out, and her little bow mouth turned down.

He backed up. "Hey, pretty baby, none of that. You'll put a black mark on my reputation with the females.''

Dora Watkins arched a brow at him.

Well, hell. He was a nervous wreck —a state he didn't like at all. What did she expect?

Hoping to cover his turmoil, he grinned at both her and the baby. And just that quickly, Katie mimicked the gesture, showing eight tiny teeth. She'd gone from cloudy to sunshine in a blink.

And though he was confused and off balance, felt

as though his whole world had been turned upside down, Ethan fell instantly and totally headlong in love.

"She's a sweetheart," he said softly. "Happy. Amanda did a good job with her."

Dora rubbed Katie's back and straightened the flounce of the frilly dress, unable to resist showing her off. "Yes." The admission elicited an odd mix of pride and pain. Dora had had as much influence on this child's disposition as Amanda had. Maybe more.

"What now?" Ethan asked.

"I promised Amanda that I would find you, take Katie to you, see if you...if you wanted her."

"Of course I want her. She's a Callahan. We take care of our own." His eyes held a banked panic, but his voice was resolute and strong, without even a hint of hesitation.

Dora felt a piece of her heart break. She'd loved Amanda like a sister, but deep inside she was bitterly hurt that Amanda would ask this of her, that her friend wouldn't just agree that Dora should adopt Katie, and be done with it. Dora adored Katie, had practically raised the child. Why should she have to find this man? Track him down when she was capable and more than willing to keep Katie? In fact, wanted desperately to keep her.

But Amanda had been dying. There hadn't been time for red tape and legal papers. And without those legal papers, Katie's life could well be thrust into the arms of Social Services, or worse yet, the hands of her maternal grandparents—and that was something Dora would never, ever allow to happen.

Inwardly she'd railed at what she considered an almost intolerable situation. She hadn't wanted to come here, had imagined that she could fight the system and Amanda's parents using her fierce love as a weapon. As for the one person who indeed had a legal right to the child, Dora had rationalized that what Ethan Callahan didn't know wouldn't hurt him.

But Dora was honest to a fault and knew she'd move heaven and earth to honor her promise to Amanda.

However, that didn't mean she would arbitrarily turn the baby over to this cowboy. No matter how strongly he'd stated his intention and desire to have his daughter.

She stared at the loosened ends of his tie and nodded. "Fine then. Which one of these trucks is yours?"

He frowned at the question, then his sexy smile tipped slightly. "None of them. The fine-looking 'Vette over there is mine."

"Figures. I doubt that souped-up cracker box will hold a state-approved car seat."

"Darlin', you shouldn't malign a man's car. It hurts his ego." He wiggled his fingers at the baby, but Katie ducked her head shyly into Dora's neck. He peeked at her and made a goofy face, and Katie grinned around her thumb, her eyes sleepy.

"I don't think your ego's in any danger—unless of course you can't get it to fit inside that sports car."

He grinned. "Are we going somewhere?"

"Home?" she suggested with a lift of her brows.

"In case you've forgotten, I *did* just pay seven thousand dollars for you."

"About that. I appreciate what you did. And I'll write you a reimbursement check. Unless you want me to go back in there and take care of it right now?"

"Afraid mine'll bounce?"

"I don't mean to offend, darlin', but not everybody keeps that sort of balance in their checking account."

She patted his cheek. "Don't worry. I'm good for it."

That surprised him. Just who was Dora Watkins? "Still, whether you can afford it or not, it's obvious you didn't come here to buy a date." He ran a fingertip over Katie's baby-soft, pudgy arm. She was nearly asleep against Dora's chest. "I'll pay you back."

She shrugged. "Suit yourself. I'll follow you."

Her confidence and sass intrigued him. And though he was still reeling from finding out he had a daughter—and imagined he'd be even more so later when it truly hit him—this sexy woman set off his innate flirting antennae.

"In my most cherished fantasies, I'd never imagined my auction date would be so eager to spend the night."

"Oh, I'll be spending more than just one night, cowboy."

"Ah, shacking up. Even better."

"You're pushing it, ace."

"Ethan," he said softly, stroking a finger down her cheek.

She went perfectly still. "What?"

He grinned at the breathy word. He'd surprised her. He liked seeing her off balance. Liked that he'd done the unsettling. Turnabout was fair play since she'd definitely set *him* off balance. "My name's Ethan."

Her powers of recovery were quick and amazing. His grin widened when she stepped back out of reach.

"I know what your name is. And you can quit with the flirting. I'm not affected."

"Liar."

"That's the second time tonight you've called me that. I don't think I like it."

"I'll apologize for the first one. But not the second." His raised brow dared her to challenge.

She ceded with a nod. "We've come a long way…Ethan. The baby's tired and so am I. I made a promise to Amanda, and part of that promise was that I stick around and make sure Katie's properly cared for, that you *want* to care for her."

"I've told you I do."

"Easy words to hand out when she's sleeping like an angel. You talk to me a month from now, after you've been through teething and crying spells and diapers and spit-up and juice dribbles on your carpet."

She had no way of knowing how her words hit him. He knew all about a kid being tossed away because he made a mess or too much noise, or simply because he was an annoying burden to adult freedom, a cramp in their lifestyle.

There was no way in hell a child of his would fall into any of those categories. Oh, he knew it wouldn't be easy. What did he know about babies or raising kids, anyway? He and his brothers ran a huge ranch outside of town. They had purebred horses, an impressive herd of cattle, flashy vehicles, airplanes, a helicopter and state-of-the-art entertainment equipment—all the toys big boys love.

But on this, Ethan knew that his brothers would agree. There was no question over accepting responsibility. Katie was a Callahan. And the Callahans took care of their own.

IF SOMEONE HAD TOLD ETHAN he'd be bringing home a woman and baby from the bachelor auction, he'd have informed them they were deluded. But that's just what he was doing.

He checked the rearview mirror as he turned down the paved drive that led to the main house, making sure Dora Watkins's minivan was still following.

White wood fences glowed silver in the moonlight, as did the house and outbuildings. White was such a clean color, neat, organized, familiar...solid. It was the first impression that had struck him when Fred Callahan had driven up this same drive twenty-six years ago, beneath the arched gateway that proclaimed Callahan Farm, home of world-famous quarter horses. Cloud-white surrounded by miles of vivid green grass.

A place where three young, scared boys could heal and grow.

The day Fred Callahan had changed the name placard over the gate to Callahan & Sons was the day Ethan and his brothers knew they were safe at last, that they'd never again have to live in fear of being dumped beside the road like unwanted kittens.

"I wish you were still here, Dad," he murmured, his soft words whipped away by the sweet evening breeze that blew through the 'Vette's open widow. Pancreatic cancer had taken Fred Callahan four years ago. It was a loss Ethan still felt keenly. "I could use some of your steady advice."

He pulled up in front of the five-thousand-square-foot house he and his brothers shared, stopping in the circular driveway. He would put the 'Vette in the garage later.

He got out and nearly had a heart attack when Dora barreled up behind him, coming within inches of his shiny, custom-painted, dent-free sports car.

Security lights illuminated her face as she popped out of the van, standing on the running board, arms folded across the top of the open door. "Nice house."

Well, I hope so, he thought, wondering what it would take to impress this woman. And why he wanted to impress her in the first place. He wasn't normally a man to brag. Perhaps it was the sassy way she'd told him she could afford to pay seven grand for a night with him.

More than one night, he reminded himself, getting an attack of nerves all over again. Who would have thought that in the space of about three hours his life would be altered so drastically. That a sweet-faced woman with long legs and a smart mouth would present him with a daughter?

A daughter.

He took a breath to steady himself. "You going to come inside, speed racer?"

She grinned at him. "My daddy says I'm the only one in the whole state of Montana who can get a ticket when there aren't even any legal speed limits."

"You like to go fast. My kind of woman."

She gave him a direct look that had his blood heating. "Are you flirting with me, Ethan Callahan?"

"I believe I am, Dora Watkins."

She grinned. "By tomorrow you'll be so busy you won't even remember your own name much less how to flirt."

He put his hands at her waist, lifted her down from the van, liking the way her trim body fitted against his. "Then we ought to make the most out of tonight, don't you think?"

Dora licked her lips. For the life of her, she couldn't move. He was smooth. So incredibly, sensually smooth. And she found that she wasn't a woman who could resist all that charm.

She'd known he was good-looking. Amanda had described him. But the reality was so much better. Brown hair shot through with gold, a movie-star face that was the epitome of masculinity. Blue eyes filled with mischief one minute and fiery seduction the next.

Her hands came to rest on the firm muscles of his arms that flexed beneath the expensive fabric of his tuxedo. An Armani if she wasn't mistaken. Grandpa owned one, and so did her brother Joe.

He lowered his head, and at that moment Dora thought she'd just die if he didn't close that distance and kiss her. But common sense was stronger than hormones.

She slapped a palm on his chest. "You get the portable crib, I'll get the baby."

"The...?"

He looked confused. "Forget about your daughter already, ace?" Good, she thought. She didn't want him to want this child. Well, she wanted him to like Katie—who could resist this precious little girl?—she just preferred that he would agree to admire her from afar.

"No, I didn't forget. You have a baby bed in there?"

"A portable one. Among other things. I told you, I came prepared to stay the month."

He nodded. "I appreciate it. It must be hard for Katie, losing her mother. Introducing her to a father she's never been around might be too confusing. It'll be best that we ease her into the household. I imagine it'll be easier since she's still so young."

"I imagine," Dora muttered, leaning in to unstrap the sleeping baby from her car seat. "Grab a couple of those suitcases, too, if you can manage."

This little dynamo was rough on a man's ego. Of course he could manage a couple of suitcases. Hadn't she just been squeezing his muscles?

"Bossy, aren't you. And I don't see anything back here that remotely resembles a crib."

Dora lifted the padded bar of the car seat and tried not to smile at the petulance in his tone. She'd pricked his masculinity, and it was just what he deserved. He was entirely too potent to the female population.

"It's that oblong blue thing with the handle."

"You're kidding."

"Trust me. It's bigger than it looks." She put a blanket around Katie and waited for Ethan to get their things and lead the way into the house. "And as for my bossiness, in my household I learned young that timidity would get you stepped on."

"You were mistreated?" He came to an abrupt halt on the first step of the porch, his voice now deadly serious.

She laughed softly, patting Katie's back when she stirred. "No. I have four brothers."

"Ah, that explains it." He muscled open the door without dropping a single thing. "Should we set up this little contraption down here or in one of the rooms?"

She arched a brow. "One of the rooms would be nice."

"Yeah. Okay. I wasn't thinking. I've never had a baby before." *Shut up, Ethan.* Disgusted with himself, he took the stairs two at a time. How did this woman keep getting the better of him? He was used to calling the shots, used to being the one who did the seducing.

Yet one look from those lake-blue eyes and he was reduced to a babbling idiot. It was going to stop.

He took them to the guest room two doors down from his own room. The walls were painted yellow, and he decided that was the perfect color for a baby's room. He would have to shift some furniture, put the bed in the attic, make a trip to the city for a crib.

My God, he was scared out of his mind.

His head spinning, he undid the portable contraption. Dora had laid Katie on the double bed and was already rifling through one of the suitcases, presumably for pajamas. Since her back was turned, he sneaked a peek at the crib assembly directions some clever soul had the extreme good sense to paste discreetly on the bottom. Probably a man, he decided. It wouldn't do to have fathers appear incompetent with something as simple as assembling a portable crib.

Now, ask him to hook up a stereo, fly a plane or pick out a prime piece of horseflesh, and he would excel.

Pleased with himself once he had the little bed all opened out and had shaken it to test for sturdiness, he went to stand by Dora. She had Katie cradled in her arms now, humming softly, coaxing the child back to sleep. It was a sight he'd never seen before, had no experience with, but one that touched him.

"I'll take your cases to your room."

"This one's fine," she whispered.

"No sense in either one of you being cramped or disturbed. We've got more bedrooms in this house than we know what to do with."

She nodded and continued to hum. The love on her face was clear to see.

He wanted to know about her relationship with Amanda, wanted to thank her for taking care of his child. He knew only too well that not everyone would welcome the responsibilities of a child thrust on them. Oh, maybe at first—and a baby was certainly hard to resist. But babies grew up, and people changed their minds.

Even biological parents.

His daughter would never have to worry about whether or not she was wanted.

He watched as Dora laid the sleeping baby in the crib and covered her with a blanket, her hand lingering over the child's back, brushing softly over her wispy hair. Without the pink dress, the baby could have been either gender.

Dora straightened and looked at him, appeared surprised that he was still there.

"I'll show you to your room," he said quietly.

"If it's next door, I imagine I can find the way."

"I imagine. But my daddy taught me to be hospitable."

"Then by all means, lead the way. I wouldn't want to corrupt your teachings."

He grinned. Damned if he didn't like her.

He set her suitcase on the settee by the window. A freestanding mahogany mirror reflected their images beside the four-poster bed with its ivory chenille spread.

"Nice," Dora said. "For a bachelor pad, the place is very well put together."

"My dad had a decorator come in. Said there was no reason we had to live like swine."

She shook her head. "For some reason, I just can't picture you living like a swine."

"Ah, compliments. I'm partial to them."

She laughed. "That was an observation, not a compliment."

"Your nose is growing, legs."

Her laughter sputtered and she choked. "Legs?"

He gave her a friendly clap on the back. "Yeah. You've got long ones...for such a little thing."

She poked a finger in his chest and had him backing up. "Careful who you call little."

He captured her fingers, flattened her palm against his chest, held it there. Her blue eyes went curious, hot and stunned. And a little unsure.

The lady liked to talk a big game, but she could be rattled.

"I wonder," he murmured, "if that mouth would feel as clever as the words that come out of it."

There. Her breath had stopped. He lowered his head, stopped just bare inches from her lips, kept his gaze on hers. He could seduce her. Would love to try. "Tell me something, legs."

Her gaze shifted from his lips to his eyes. She nodded slightly.

"Where did you learn those bidding skills you displayed earlier?"

He toyed with her hair, felt his heart bump when she tilted her chin, brushed her lower body against his, deliberately. Her blue eyes filled with amusement as well as curious desire.

"I've had plenty of practice at church auctions."

"Mmm." He wasn't sure what she found so amusing, but he was a man who could make a woman forget her name if he chose to. And right this minute the chemistry was ripe in the room and he chose to.

His lips were a sigh away from contact, his libido a millisecond away from combustion.

"At my daddy's church," she added.

Her breath was warm against his lips, firing his fantasies. "Your daddy's—"

The mirth in her eyes and her tone had his brain screaming "whoa!" He dropped his hands and leaped back as though he'd been goosed with a branding iron. His hip rammed against the marble corner of the dresser top.

"You're a preacher's daughter?" It came out as an accusation.

"Is that a problem?"

The little wench was doing her best not to laugh at him. "Yes, it's a problem. I nearly seduced you right here in the bedroom."

A preacher's daughter. In his book that put her right up there with the nuns.

Off-limits for a sinner like him.

But, man alive, this particular preacher's daughter was something else. She had the look of an angel...and made him think of pure sin.

"Oh, believe me, cowboy. You were a *long* way from seducing me."

Chapter Three

As challenges went, that one was blatant. Ethan nearly stepped forward to show her exactly how wrong she was—that he could indeed seduce her in two seconds flat and have her begging for more.

Then he reminded himself just who was challenging him here.

He raked a hand through his hair. "I need a drink. And I need to get out of this bedroom."

"I've made you nervous."

His brows slammed down. "Definitely. And I'm not too proud to admit it."

"Mmm. A man who's in touch with his feelings."

"I didn't say anything about emotions."

"A prude, then?"

"Woman, you're testing my limits. And that's tough to do, since I'm well aware of them and pride myself on strict control."

"And your control doesn't extend to a preacher's daughter?"

"Are you baiting me?"

"Evidently I am. And I haven't the slightest idea

why." She laughed at herself. "We've really gotten off track here. But you're so cute when you're flustered."

"Cute?" He shook his head. "Will you join me downstairs? I have questions."

This brought an end to the teasing. Dora nodded. "I figured you would." She followed him out of the room and down the stairs.

The house was huge and tastefully decorated in neutral colors. Clean and organized, she decided, yet the quality of the furnishings and art on the walls gave a subtle hint of wealth.

Dora wasn't awed by wealth. She had her own fortune and was comfortable either in a mansion or a three-room apartment.

"You said just you and your brothers live here?"

"Yes. Why?"

"It's so…" She waved a hand. "Orderly."

"My brothers—Grant and Clay—and I all have the same type of personality. I guess that's why we get along so well."

"You might want to prepare yourself for a personality change. A baby will do that, you know."

It seemed she was testing him, almost hoping he would complain. That reminded him that he knew very little about her or the baby. Or Amanda for that matter.

He stepped behind the wet bar and watched as she wandered around the entertainment room. It was his favorite in the house, measuring thirty by twenty feet with all the latest state-of-the-art equipment.

She touched a panel and shrieked as the bookcase

slid back and turned electronically to reveal his coveted twenty-thousand-dollar stereo system.

With her hand to her bosom she glared at him. "What is this? Batman's cave?"

He grinned. "Like it?"

"It nearly gave me a coronary. How did that happen?"

"You touched the sensor. It's just there." He pointed to the corner she'd been trailing her fingers over. "It's touch sensitive. Your body heat'll activate it."

"Is there a way to turn it off?"

"Sure. With the remote."

"Then I suggest you use it. Katie will likely climb up on the shelf and get swept away in the cave. We'll never find her."

He hadn't thought of that. But then, why should he? He hadn't had babies in the house. Other than his godson, Timmy Malone, before he'd died. And Stony Stratton's daughter, Nikki. This was an adult male household. He'd never had to think about safety precautions.

He did now, pressing the remote button that would lock out the sensor and keep the movable wall in place.

"Does she walk?"

"Not yet. But she's quicker than lightning on all fours, fearless and part monkey."

He belted back the scotch in his glass and poured another. "Want one?"

"No, thanks."

He kept forgetting she was a preacher's daughter.

It stood to reason she wouldn't drink or cuss or…oh, man, no sex, either. He didn't know if he was going to survive. Her face alone could make him forget his mind. Those legs…well, he wasn't even going to go there.

"You said you were going to stay a month?"

"At least."

He nearly groaned.

She reached out a hand to caress his stereo equipment and the smooth wood that housed it, then hesitated, looking at him over her shoulder. Her derriere in tight jeans was fueling his fantasies.

"Is it going to do its haunted house thing if I touch?"

"No. I turned it off."

She did caress then, making him sweat. Hell, it was stereo components, for crying out loud. She stroked them as if they were male body parts.

"My brothers would drool over this."

In this discussion he was on much firmer ground. "It's designed to make grown men drool. The four hundred watt speakers alone will make a man salivate."

She smiled. "You don't consider that a bit of overkill?"

"Are you kidding?" A person couldn't have too much wattage.

"Mmm, loud enough to take care of your house and your neighbor's, too."

He grinned. "Good thing they're five miles away."

"With four hundred watts blaring, I imagine they

can sit on their porch and save their own electricity bill.''

''In that case I'm helping my neighbors balance their household budget.''

''And ruining your children's ears in the process.''

''I don't have children.''

She arched a brow. ''How soon we forget.''

The reminder slammed into his gut and had his hands trembling. He sat down on the ivory leather sectional sofa, a large piece of furniture that was virtually swallowed by the size of the room.

''Despite what you might think, I'm careful and considerate in relationships.''

''Not too careful with Amanda.''

''No. She caught me off guard. She said she was using birth control.''

''She would. When she made up her mind about something, she acted on it, often a bit impulsively.''

''She wanted to get pregnant?''

''No.'' Dora leaned against a recliner chair, but didn't sit. ''She wanted to feel special that night. Wanted it badly enough to mislead you, to pretend you cared.''

Ethan winced. He'd felt a fondness for Amanda, but beyond that it had been two consenting adults sharing a sophisticated night of intimacy with no illusions or pretenses. He'd known she was using him to soothe, but he hadn't asked her for what.

And he'd broken his number-one cardinal rule. He'd created a child out of wedlock. A child very much like himself, who had never known his father.

Except Dora Watkins had the compassion to

change that for Katie. He appreciated it more than he could say. Even though finding out he had a daughter was a terrifying jolt to his life, would take adjustments he hadn't planned on, he would rather know now than find out years down the road—years that could have possibly held heartache and ruin for an innocent child.

"I'm ashamed to say I didn't even know Amanda's last name."

"Bishop."

"What made her give Katie my name? If she didn't plan to tell me about the baby?"

"I don't know. She wanted Katie. The baby was someone who would love her unconditionally. You know, that was the only thing Amanda and I ever fussed about—her self-esteem. Anyway, the night she met you, she'd just had a run-in with her parents— I'm sorry to say the Bishops are truly misguided, lost people—and I honestly think Amanda was feeling a little rebellious."

"So why didn't she contact me when she learned about the baby?"

"She didn't know you. And after the fact, she was ashamed to admit she'd had a one-night affair. As it was, when she told her folks about the baby, they didn't want anything to do with her. Her behavior contradicted their traditional values." There was more than a little snap in her tone.

"Some people don't deserve to be parents."

"Yes, that's very sad but true. It always amazed me how happy Amanda was, what a fun person she was, given the environment she grew up in. The min-

ute we graduated from high school, we got an apartment together. I can't remember a day that went by
that she didn't have me rolling on the floor laughing.
That's the way she was."

"My dad used to say laughter was a gift."

"It is," Dora agreed. "And Amanda was truly
gifted. She worked at the church and she loved her
job, and Dad loved having her, but after Katie was
born, she decided she needed to look for something
that paid better. She was my best friend, and I could
certainly afford to support them, or at least supple-
ment her income, but Amanda was proud. In fact, she
was coming back from a job interview when the accident happened." Her voice wobbled, and she swallowed hard. "I was keeping Katie when we got the
call."

"I'm sorry." The words seemed inadequate. And
empty. He hadn't known the woman, yet he'd had a
child with her. For that reason alone he felt a sadness
at the loss. And despite the fact that there'd been no
contact between him and Amanda after that night, he
hadn't forgotten her. She hadn't been a faceless body.
He wanted to tell Dora this, but she was speaking
again.

"She was still alive when I got to the hospi-
tal…and that's when she asked me to find you." Dora
looked away. She wasn't ready to tip her hand and
tell him how much she wanted Katie for herself, to
tell him that her true agenda was to get him to sign
adoption rights to the baby she loved as her own.
"She didn't want her parents to raise Katie."

"If they turned their back on their own daughter,

why would they want the burden of a granddaughter?''

"Oh, they didn't want the burden. They wanted money.''

"From who?''

"Me. They knew how close Amanda and I were, and that I'd do anything for her. They were aware of how Amanda felt about them, that she didn't want them to influence or ruin her daughter's life.''

"She told them that?''

"Once. A few months back when they'd run into one another on the street. So at the funeral they offered to sell the baby to me.''

Ethan swore, then glanced up and apologized.

"Don't apologize. I feel exactly the same way.''

"Well, with me in the picture, they don't have a legal right to Katie.''

"That's exactly why Amanda named you on the birth certificate.''

"I'm glad she did.''

Dora was, too. To a point. This whole situation was new to Ethan, and she could see how after hearing Amanda's story he'd likely be thinking with emotional stars in his eyes with regard to Katie's fate and future. It would be best to let the day-to-day reality of living with a baby give him a good shaking up. Then she could ease him around to her way of thinking.

Though she doubted she'd have much trouble there when all was said and done. This was the least likely household for a baby, an all-male ranch house that spoke of wealth with touches of James Bond. He would see that soon enough. Before the month was up, he'd be asking her to let him sign over adoption papers.

He stood and stepped toward her, reaching out to tip up her chin. "Thank you for bringing Katie to me," he said softly.

The turmoil inside her was like a swirling vortex. She didn't know this man, but she responded to him. And that was dangerous. She had an agenda. He was part of the short term, not the long term.

She stepped back out of reach. "I think I'll turn in now, if you don't mind."

"There's one more thing I was wondering."

"What?"

"How did you happen to find out about the auction?"

"That was pure accident. I confided in my dad after the funeral about Amanda's last wishes. Turns out he knew Ozzie and called ahead to make sure I wouldn't be walking into a dangerous situation or something."

Ethan looked affronted.

Dora shrugged. "What can I say? He's protective. Anyway, Dad said Ozzie was expecting me to meet him at Brewer's Saloon."

Ethan stared a moment, then his brows rose. "That old goat. It was a setup."

"Excuse me?"

"The old fellas have been planning this auction for a reason. They're on some crazy marriage campaign here. They roped a buddy of mine just last month."

"But you intend to escape," she guessed astutely.

"Exactly. I'm not interested in commitment."

THE NEXT MORNING, Ethan was on his way downstairs when an unfamiliar noise stopped him.

The babbling sound of a baby.

How could he have forgotten? He wasn't alone in the house. This wasn't a day like any of the others before in his life.

He had a baby daughter.

And a beautiful house guest.

Cautiously he peered into the yellow room and couldn't stop the smile that pulled at his lips. Little Katie was standing up in the portable crib, her tiny hands gripping the plastic rail.

Ethan moved closer. "Hi."

She did a little jumping dance, her pudgy knees bending as she held on to the side of the small crib.

"I can see this thing's not gonna corral you for much longer." He paused, his heart flipping when she smiled and babbled at him.

"I'm your daddy." He had no idea why he'd blurted that out, knew she wouldn't understand. And saying it aloud made him feel as if he was going to hyperventilate. The responsibility was enormous.

He tested the title, said it again. It felt right. He held out his hands. "Want out of that cage?"

She stopped her knee bends, appeared to consider. Then her sunny disposition that tickled him so took over and she smiled and gave a happy shriek.

"I guess that's a yes." He lifted her, felt the warm wetness soak into his shirt, belatedly smelled the soggy diaper. "Whoa, you're a mess."

"Need some help?"

He whipped around and nearly lost his hold on the

little girl. Once she saw Dora her squeal became louder and she extended her arms, nearly wiggling right out of his embrace.

"Morning," Ethan said softly. Man alive, her allure was even more potent in the light of day. It was going to be difficult to remember that this woman was only a temporary guest, that she was off-limits. "Katie wanted out of her pen."

"She told you that, hmm?" Dora moved into the room and took the baby, nuzzling her sweet-smelling cheek. When she'd seen Ethan with Katie in his arms, she'd been horribly jealous. This was *her* baby. She didn't want to share. She didn't want them to form a bond. And that was ugly.

"Well, she was talking up a storm about something."

Dora smiled. He was dressed in well-worn jeans, boots and a shirt that lovingly hugged his incredibly broad shoulders. Last night he'd been a vision in black tie. This morning he was the epitome of a sexy cowboy. And it was ridiculous how the sight of him made her heart pound and her hands tremble. Used to being around men, she wasn't normally affected by macho types.

This one defied the norm.

"You can usually make out about every tenth word."

"Ah, a challenge. Just like a female." He picked up Katie's little hand and brought it to his lips, kissed it gallantly, then pretended to gnaw, eliciting shrieks of laughter.

Dora found her footing. She could deal with the

flirty cowboy side of him. It was the vulnerable one she had trouble with.

"Well, if you'll excuse us, this female appears to need a diaper change."

"Mmm, privacy. If you'll tell me where you put your keys, I'll unload your van."

"I've already taken care of it."

"Early riser?"

"Always. Each day is too precious not to appreciate. I rarely miss greeting the sun."

She was an enigma. How could one woman emanate such sex appeal and still appear as innocent as a dew-kissed rose?

He needed to get out of this room—this *bedroom*—before his thoughts went off on a tangent that they had no business exploring.

Since she'd already turned to gather clothes for the baby, Ethan took himself downstairs...and nearly toppled off the last flight of stairs.

His normally pristine house looked as though a tornado had hit it. For a moment he was simply too stunned to move.

Dora had very definitely and very obviously gotten up early to unload her van. Toys and...*stuff* were all over the place.

The front door opened, and Ethan looked up as his brothers Grant and Clay came in. They, too, came to a screeching halt.

"Holy smoke. Did somebody throw a fit in here or what?" Grant asked.

Ethan moved the rest of the way into the foyer, but

before he could answer, Dora came downstairs with Katie in her arms.

Grant and Clay stared.

"Some auction," Clay whispered with a reverence that had Ethan wanting to deck him.

"I take it these are the brothers?" Dora asked.

"Yes. Dora Watkins, meet Grant and Clay." He looked at his brothers, annoyed at the awestruck, rapt expressions on their faces. Never mind that he, too, tended to get stupid when she so much as walked into a room. His brothers needed to be brought up to speed lest they inadvertently offend. They were just as susceptible to flirting with a gorgeous female as the next man.

"Her daddy's a *preacher.*"

She smiled and shot him an indulgent look. "I'll see that declaration, Ethan, and raise you. Guys, this is Katie. Ethan's daughter."

Both Grant and Clay whipped their heads around so fast it was a wonder their hats stayed on. Ethan was trying to decide how he felt about her using gambling analogies to introduce his baby.

"You made a *preacher's daughter* pregnant?" Grant's tone was filled with horrified accusation. "What the hell—heck's—the matter with you?"

"I did no such thing. I've got some scruples. It was her friend."

"*Who* was her friend?" Clay asked.

"Katie's mother."

"Was *she* a preacher's daughter, too?" Grant wanted to know.

Ethan looked at Dora for that one. It shamed him

to realize he'd made a baby with a woman and didn't know a thing about her except what Dora had told him last night. And despite the nasty picture Dora had painted of Amanda's parents, one never knew.

Dora shook her head. "Nope. Only one daughter in the Watkins household. And that's me. But don't any of you think you've got to treat me like a nun or something. Try it and I'll put salt in the sugar bowl or loosen the cinch on your saddles." She grinned to let them know she was teasing. "I've got four brothers, and I know how to hold my own. Right now, though, I'm starving, and so's Katie."

Like a whirlwind she headed for the kitchen as though she was intimately familiar with the lay of the house, stepping right over the mess as she went. Surely she saw the tripping hazards.

Ethan and his brothers followed, each of them gathering up toys, suitcases, clothes and camera equipment, stopping to look at each another. "Where should we put it?" Grant asked.

Ethan shrugged. "I don't know. Dora's room, maybe?"

"What about the toys?"

"I guess we could set up the library as a play-room."

"Babies can tear pages out of books."

Ethan shot Clay an annoyed look. "She's barely one. We won't be leaving her alone in there."

"Oh, good point."

"Let's just leave the stuff for now," Grant suggested.

They agreed as one and followed Dora to the

kitchen. She had her head poked in the subzero re-frigerator. Katie was happily making a racket by kick-ing her feet against the metal footrest of a high chair. Where the heck had that come from? Had *all* this stuff fitted inside that minivan?

He looked back at Dora. She was wearing another pair of those figure-hugging jeans that molded her derriere and made him think of pure sin. He noticed that Grant's and Clay's tongues were all but hanging out, and he gave Grant a shove, knocking him into Clay. "Cut it out."

"Mmm-hmm," Grant hummed quietly. "Looks like a certain playboy's ga-ga over the preacher's daughter."

"Shut up, Grant."

"Pretty impressive fridge, guys," Dora said. "How about some eggs?"

"Sure." As long as she would quit bending over like that, he'd agree to just about anything.

"Katie likes them scrambled, so that's what you'll get." She set about cracking eggs in a bowl, tossing the shells toward the sink, dribbling egg whites across the countertop and down the face of the cabinets. Ethan expected her to get a rag and wipe up the mess. He was a clean-as-you-go type of cook. Obviously Dora wasn't. She didn't even appear to realize she was slinging white goo over his shiny granite and polished oak.

He went over and took care of the mess himself, put the top back on the can of nonstick spray.

She glanced at him and smiled. "You can do the

toast if you like. If you want meat to go with the eggs, you're on your own. Katie'll get impatient.''

"Eggs and toast will be fine."

"I'll do it," Clay volunteered, making a valiant effort to keep the cringe from his voice. The kitchen was pretty much Clay's domain.

Ethan nearly smiled at the bewildered, helplessly stunned expression on his youngest brother's face as he watched the haphazard manner in which Dora was systematically destroying the huge, gourmet ranch kitchen.

Clay was nearly as proud of the restaurant-grade stove and grill as they all were of their stereo equipment and purebred horses.

Katie banged a spoon against the plastic tray of her high chair, and all three men came to a halt, each turning to look at the baby.

Dora scooped eggs out of the pan and spread them on the plate to cool, glancing at the three men who were so intrigued by the baby. She wondered if it was the heat from the stove that made her so hot, then had to admit that the sinfully good looks of the Callahan brothers—Ethan in particular—had more to do with the heat than a gas flame. All of them were dark-haired and broad-shouldered with faces that might have been carved by a world-famous sculptor. The testosterone alone in the room was enough to delight a crowd of women in their prime.

And though Dora considered herself in her prime, she told herself she would not be affected. Especially by Ethan Callahan.

She shouldered her way between them to feed Katie her eggs. "The toast is burning."

Clay swore.

"Language," Ethan and Grant admonished in unison.

Clay apologized, then charged across the room to rescue the bread before the smoke alarm went off.

Dora rolled her eyes. "You guys are going to get on my nerves."

Grant sat at the table to observe, and Ethan hovered close, watching every spoonful that Dora shoveled into Katie's smiling mouth. The baby managed to grab a handful of mushy eggs and squish them through her fingers.

"Sit, would you?" Dora suggested. "Katie'll get indigestion with you staring at her like that."
Ethan obeyed without thinking.

Clay set plates of eggs and toast on the table, then wiped up the floor beneath the high chair just as Max nosed his way in the kitchen. The golden retriever looked as bewildered as the Callahans felt, but recovered quicker when he noticed the eggs being slung on the floor.

Katie squealed at the sight of the dog, and Dora beamed.

"Oh, he's beautiful!"

"Max." Ethan snapped his fingers, halting the dog in midlick. "Show some manners."

Katie reached over the side of the high chair, and Dora grabbed her hand, carefully introducing the dog and baby. Ethan realized she was accustomed to animals. The baby appeared so, too.

"He's a big dog. I'm surprised she's not afraid."

"Oh, Katie's grown up with animals. I've usually got a menagerie around me. I photograph them."

"That explains the camera equipment I saw in the hall."

She nodded and shoveled more eggs in Katie's mouth, practically becoming a contortionist, since the baby was still intent on playing with the dog. "Is he the only one, or do you have more?"

"Dogs?"

"Yes."

"Justine and a pup. The neighbors talked us out of the other puppies."

"Oh, too bad. Who named the mama dog?"

"That would be Grant's doing. Reminded him of a girlfriend."

She raised a brow. "She looked like a dog?"

Grant grinned, showing her that his smile could be almost as potent as his brother's. "No, she had beautiful yellow hair and graceful limbs."

"Ah, you based it on sex."

"Now, I didn't say that," Grant sputtered. At the same time Ethan said, "Would you not be talking that way?"

"You guys really are going to have to get past my father's vocation or we're going to have a lot of trouble living together."

"Living…?" Grant couldn't seem to finish his sentence, and Clay knocked over his chair in the midst of trying to sit on it.

Ethan sighed. This maddening, unpredictable, energetic woman was about to set them all on their ears and turn their household into chaos. He owed it to his brothers to let them know.

"Dora's moving in with us for a month."

Chapter Four

Dora spent the next few days getting acclimated to her new living quarters. The ranch was gorgeous, all flowing green grass, pristine fences and high-tech stables that housed horses whose bloodlines were legendary.

The Callahans dabbled in quite a few ventures, it seemed. Horses, cattle, stock markets. Their equipment was top-notch, their white pickups polished to a shine with the Callahan & Sons name and logo emblazoned in dark green. The green-and-white color scheme and logo were proudly displayed on stable blankets, buckets, towels and every other implement as a stamp of ownership and advertisement. Everything had its place and gleamed, showing at first glance that this was a wealthy and well-run operation.

Dora was impressed—though she was careful not to let on to Ethan. It tickled her to see his pique when she appeared unmoved by his efforts to dazzle her. And he really didn't have to try very hard. Just looking at him was enough to render her speechless. He deserved every bit of his playboy reputation.

With her camera hanging around her neck and Katie strapped in a backpack, Dora poked around in the barn and decided she'd landed in the middle of an animal gold mine. An old barn cat had a litter of kittens that were just precious. Dora could already envision the shot she'd get of the tiger-fur babies peeking out of a ten-gallon hat.

Now if she could just talk one of these cowboys out of theirs, she'd be in good shape.

The eerie scream of a horse snagged her attention, the sound pulling at something deep inside her she didn't understand.

"What was that?" Dora asked Katie.

Like a little parrot, Katie whispered, "S'sat?"

Ever curious, Dora followed the noise to one of the outbuildings where the hive of activity had her raising her camera and clicking shots for the pure pleasure of it.

"Oh, my," she said, her voice barely audible. Katie appeared similarly awestruck because she didn't try to repeat the words.

A magnificent, jet-black stallion, head lifted, nostrils flaring, mane shifting in the breeze was being led into a large indoor paddock where a pretty, gleaming chestnut mare waited in a special stall, her breast against the railing, her tail wrapped and held to the side by Ethan's brother, Clay. Grant was handling the stallion and Ethan was giving directions to his brothers in a soft, deep voice.

A breeding shed, she realized, with a breeding in progress.

Dora had been around animals all her life, but she'd

never seen the mating rituals of horses up close and personal this way.

Fascinated, a bit embarrassed, she watched as the mare appeared to ready herself, shifting restlessly. Eagerly.

She saw Ethan grin as though he were a warrior celebrating a victory. Muscles rippled and bunched in his arms as he helped Grant control the quivering stallion who appeared more than willing to get to the main event.

"Easy does it, now," he crooned. "Let's show the lady a good time."

Dora's cheeks heated before she realized he was talking about the mare, not her. He didn't even know she was standing there.

The mare, though hobbled and covered with a blanket of leather for protection, regally tossed her head and gave a call of submission just as the stallion lunged and covered her. It was a wild, powerful, awesome sight, and Dora was riveted...and strangely aroused.

She must have drawn in a breath, or perhaps it was Katie's little voice that got his attention, because at that moment Ethan looked at her.

For several seconds she couldn't move. Their gazes locked, and a fine sexual tension arced between them like buzzing electricity, sending her blood roaring in her ears. The power of that intense, exclusive look whipped through her, robbing her of breath and thought. Erotic images she knew little about melded with the sounds and scents of animals, nature and sex.

Then Katie broke the spell by aptly putting her little hands over Dora's eyes. Ethan laughed, and Dora pulled away Katie's hands in time to see him physically assisting the horses in their coupling.

Appalled, fascinated, she couldn't look away. The power of it all had her heart racing. The air palpitated with strength and frenzied need and an edgy, elemental violence that seduced even as it frightened.

Once again Ethan turned and caught her stare. He appeared as magnetized and confused as she was by this obvious and strange force that seemed to hold them.

With a slight frown he spoke to his brothers, then made his way toward Dora and Katie, taking care to stay out of the way of the mating animals who were now being led away from each other.

"Come out to get an education on the birds and the bees?" he asked, urging Dora away from the paddock. He flicked a finger against Katie's cheek, causing the baby to giggle.

"I'm a bit old for lessons on the birds and bees, but I've never seen anything like that before." Her voice sounded more whiskey-coated than normal, and her breathing nearly matched those of the heaving, sweating horses. She was moved and stunned and fascinated all at once.

"It's something, isn't it?" Far enough away now, they turned and watched as Clay and Grant each took their respective horses in opposite directions, walking them to cool them down, as well as to soothe. "Those two will produce an excellent foal."

"I thought big operations like this relied on artificial insemination."

"We do both."

But today the stallion got lucky, she thought. "It seems so cold-blooded to mate purely for perfect genetics."

He shrugged. "That's what owners pay us for though. They're the bloodlines that'll win the Triple Crown."

"Do you only breed Thoroughbreds for racing?"

"No. We produce a really good line of cow ponies and pleasure horses as well."

"And you train them here, too?" She'd seen several of the cowboys riding and working with the beautiful horses.

"A few. Mostly we turn them over to a neighbor, Stony Stratton. Between my stud's bloodlines and Stony's uncanny way with the horses, we turn out some of the finest stock in the world."

"Impressive," she said before she thought to stop herself.

"Finally, I do something to impress the woman." His grin was quick and sexy.

"Don't let it go to your head, hotshot."

He looked at Katie. "Does she talk to you like this, too?" he asked the little girl.

Katie babbled and clapped her hands.

"Thankfully, Katie didn't inherit your ego. She's perfectly humble and sweet as candy."

"I'm pretty sweet." He ran a finger over Dora's lips. "Want to taste?" No sooner were the words out of his mouth than he was backtracking. "Hell—I mean, heck, I'm sorry."

This man was tough on her hormones. He went

from hot to cool in the blink of an eye. His determination to treat her with reverence was keeping her in a state of sexual flux. And that was a state she had no experience with.

He made her want to explore, then he would just pull back. It was frustrating as all get-out.

"After our bout with voyeurism, seems only natural to think about sex."

"We weren't thinking about—" He stopped, obviously flustered. "Voyeurism?"

"What else would you call it? We were watching those horses. Avidly, I might add."

"Avidly," he parroted, charming her with his discomfort.

"Yes, and I don't even know their names."

"Duke of Earl and Synchronicity."

"Doesn't it make you...hot, watching this all the time?"

"Legs, this isn't a conversation you and I should be having." He tugged his hat lower on his brow and glanced away.

"Ethan Callahan, you're a big fraud."

"If you're speaking of my notorious playboy reputation, you're right. It's highly overstated. And it's nonexistent when it comes to holy, church ladies."

"Who says I'm a church lady?"

"You did."

"I said my father was a minister."

"Same thing."

"Not at all."

For a full five seconds he stared at her. "You're

playing with fire, here. You're a lamb and I'm the big bad wolf.''

"Hmm. I wonder." A big bad wolf didn't go to such obvious lengths to resist temptation.

"Maybe we should change the subject."

"Maybe." She had no idea what had gotten into her, why she was so riveted by him, why she was so determined to tempt him in the first place. It was crazy.

And they both seemed to have forgotten that she had a baby strapped to her back.

His baby.

He examined the camera that hung around her neck. "Been taking pictures?"

"Thinking about it. I hadn't actually lined up any shots. And that reminds me. I'll need a dark room. Your upstairs laundry room will do nicely, if you don't mind."

"I've an idea my minding wouldn't make a bit of difference."

"Are you implying I'm pushy?"

His lips twitched. "You said it."

"And here I'd heard cowboys were gentlemen."

"Mmm. And so we are. Take whichever room you want. We have plenty. What is it that you do with these pictures you take?"

"I sell them to a greeting card company. Not the actual photos, but the sketches I make from them."

"And this is what pays you enough money to afford a seven-thousand-dollar donation for a date?"

"No. Quentin Watkins is why I can afford seven-thousand-dollar donations."

"Quentin Watkins?"

"My grandfather. Texas oilman. Filthy rich and he adores me."

"Little wonder." His gaze traveled over her hair, her face, rested on her lips. He took a breath. "So you don't *have* to work."

"No more than you do," she countered, her brow raised.

"Touché."

"I enjoy what I do, though. Just as I can see you do."

"Yeah." His gaze shifted to a mechanical walker where a mare happily trudged in a circle after being washed. "I love breeding horses. I even like the cattle, though that's more of a dirty, sweaty job than the horses. We've built up an operation here that pretty much ensures we can have what we want. Money will often do that. Surely you see that in your own life."

She shrugged but didn't answer right away. Because all the money in the world couldn't buy certain things.

It couldn't buy the right to a little girl who wasn't her biological daughter.

And to that end Dora realized she was going about her goal the wrong way. Ethan needed to know just how great a commitment raising a baby entailed. And he certainly wouldn't learn that if she continued to shoulder all the responsibility for Katie.

"Money can be a blessing or a curse, depending on whose hands it's in. You've obviously handled yours well. I wonder, though, how you imagine fitting

Katie into this lifestyle of having anything you want and pulling up stakes on a whim.''

''I don't pull up stakes on a whim. I'm firmly rooted in this land.''

''That's not what I meant.''

''Then clarify.''

''What are you going to do when you want to date? When you want to fly off somewhere just for the sheer foolishness of it?''

''Foolishness?''

She shrugged, tried not to smile at the affront in his voice.

''Most folks retain a trusted baby-sitter,'' he said.

''And are you going to turn over the raising of Katie to a baby-sitter?''

''I never said that.''

''What about when you're working the ranch?''

His chest expanded, and he glanced at the backpack Katie was happily bouncing in, causing Dora to steady her stance lest she be thrown off balance. ''You seem to manage.''

''It's what I've chosen. It's what I've adapted to,'' she corrected. For some reason she still didn't want him to know how desperately she wanted to keep Katie as her own. If she asked him to sign over custody right now, he'd give her an emphatic no. She was sure of it. Because it was still very new to him.

He shoved his hands in his pockets, took a step back. She wondered if he even realized the unconscious distance he'd created, then decided he didn't. The man was frightened of his child and doing his utmost not to show it.

"You're here to get us going on the right track," he reminded as though it was just that simple.

"To watch and observe. So far, I'm doing more *doing*."

Something came over his features then, like a memory that scraped him raw. "You're tired of the responsibility." His words were flat with an underlying whip to them.

"I didn't say—" She bit her tongue, wondering if she was about to make the biggest mistake of her life. In the end, though, she couldn't bring herself to let him think that she viewed Katie as a burden. "I made a promise to Amanda," she said quietly.

He tested the straps of the backpack, and a soft smile touched his lips when Katie latched on to his fingers, dragged them right into her slobbery mouth. "Here, now, sweet peach. My paws are dirty." Katie smacked and drooled even more. He looked back up at Dora. "Does this contraption come in an extra-large?"

"I imagine."

"Then let's you and me take a shopping trip. I doubt I could get one shoulder in that one."

She nearly smiled. He had that look on his face that clearly stated, "Anything you can do, I can do, too." Watching him rise to the challenge was going to be entertaining, and, never one to turn down an adventure, Dora agreed to go.

Besides, a shopping trip with the three of them would mean she would still be mainly in charge of Katie.

THE SKY WAS CLEAR and endlessly blue, the twin-engine Baron scooting along at 180 knots and handling like a dream. Katie was sound asleep, looking like an angel. Very much like the beautiful woman beside him. But despite the fact that they were soaring close to the heavens, the angel in the front seat made him think of sin.

"You don't do things by small measure, do you?" Dora asked, her voice whisky-soft through the aviation headset.

Ethan looked over at her. Her blond hair brushed her shoulders and the seat belt defined her pert breasts. And he was *not* going to notice her breasts, or anything else about her for that matter. The purpose of the trip was to shop for nursery furniture. A purely platonic outing.

Too bad Dora Watkins didn't inspire platonic thoughts.

"You mean the plane? Why should I skimp if I've got the means to do otherwise?"

"Bragger."

His grin was quick and self-assured. "Nothing wrong with that. I work hard for what I have."

"Ouch."

"No. I didn't mean to disparage your wealth, Dora."

She winked at him. "I know."

Ethan was glad they were flying instead of driving. That sexy wink would have caused him to run off the road. As it was, it sent his blood pressure spiking.

"The auctioneer the other night, Lloyd, claimed it

sinful to own more than one flashy car. Does he know about both your flashy airplanes, too?''

"Yeah, but don't forget, I share this with my brothers—if they beg real nice." He flashed his grin again. "I like hotrod planes, and mine are honeys. As for Lloyd's reference to gluttony, what can I say? I use the one eighty-five for cattle work and this Baron for pleasure."

"And shopping," Dora added.

"Mmm. Life is good." He checked his coordinates and banked left. "You mentioned something when we were talking about Amanda. You said the church couldn't afford to pay her much."

She knew what he was getting at. "People who know our background often don't understand. Despite Grandpa's millions, Daddy insists on contributing to worthwhile charities rather than the church itself. He's always claimed his own bank account isn't a charity, and since Grandpa's alive and well and ornery enough to outlive us all, there's no point in talking about premature inheritances."

"But you have a trust fund."

"I did mention that Grandpa's ornery, right?" She grinned. "He says it's his right and his duty to do as he pleases with his grandkids—unless one of us should get the calling, that is. He'll bulldoze the rest of us, but he won't mess with the Man Upstairs."

Ethan laughed. "Sounds a lot like Ozzie Peyton. Have any of you gotten the calling?"

"My brother Mike. Joe and Kenny are deacons, but that's as involved as they want to get. Same goes for Lyle. But back to your question about Amanda, a church the size of ours doesn't lend itself to enormous salaries. Plus, Amanda was proud enough to want to make her way on her own.''

"Admirable."

"She was."

"Speaking of admirable, I did actually do some research on your grandfather. Quentin Watkins is quite a man."

"You won't get an argument from me. He's a big bear of a guy with the heart of a lamb."

Ethan lifted a brow. "Somehow I don't think he'd agree with that description."

Dora laughed. "Then don't tell him I said so."

"The two of you are close."

"Mmm. I spent summers in Texas with him and Grandma. I lived there while I went to Texas U."

"What was your major?"

"Business. With a minor in arts."

"And out of that you chose photography?"

"It's what suits me. There's always something new and exciting through the lens of the camera. It captures nuances that most people are too busy to notice. Including me, which is why I use photos as a blueprint for my sketches. It's what gives me an edge."

"And you publish it for all the world to see."

"People have to stop and smell the roses sometime. In my case I use baby animals to evoke emotions, often adding a touch of the ridiculous. A cute, candid pose with the right caption can make you laugh out loud or smile softly or even bring you to tears."

"Do you write the copy?"

"No. I only draw the images."

"I'd like to see your portfolio sometime."

She grinned. "I'll be sure to invite you up to see my etchings."

The image brought about by that teasing statement made him sweat. Dora's soft laugh drifting through the headset had him jerking to face her.

"You're fun to tease—for a playboy cowboy."

"And you're awfully impertinent—for a preacher's daughter."

"Two for two."

"You're a lousy scorekeeper, legs."

"You mean we're not even? Who's winning?"

"I hate to admit it, but I'm sure you are."

"Good. I like to win." And the stakes she was aiming for were precious and very high.

She felt the plane begin its descent and looked below. Rolling hills, green from summer rains, and dense stands of pines surrounded a small brick house and a narrow private landing strip. The landscape was very different from the prairies of Shotgun Ridge that they'd left behind an hour or so ago.

"Doesn't look like an international airport or a mall to me," she commented.

Ethan's deep, masculine laughter caressed her ears through the headset. "Smart and sexy, too."

She nearly got sidetracked by the "sexy" remark. He was a man who could hand out flirty lines easily. But with her, he usually backpedaled. And as much as that often frustrated her, it also sparked her femininity. Because she realized that he did indeed find her sexy—even though he didn't want to.

The importance of his opinion surprised her. It was

something she was going to have to give some thought to. But at the moment she was too busy trying to calculate the braking distance of a streaking airplane on a small runway in the boondocks.

"Uh, are you actually planning to land down there?"

"Yep."

"Wouldn't it have been easier just to take the truck to Billings?"

"Where's your sense of adventure?"

Being the only girl with four brothers, a question like that was as good as a dare. And Dora rarely resisted a dare. "Just as strong as yours. Aim good and don't blink."

"I've got great instincts, legs. Sit back and relax."

She deliberately rested her hands in her lap, even though they wanted to fist. She would say one thing for Ethan Callahan. He kept her excitement level at a fever pitch.

When the wheels had touched ground and they were taxiing toward a man waiting beside an ancient-looking station wagon, Dora spoke again. "You know someone here who has a crib?"

"It just so happens that Scott and Shelly own a baby store in town. I like to patronize my friends' businesses whenever possible. Although I never thought I'd have the need for Treechman's Baby Land."

And Dora was hoping his need was only temporary.

Katie was awake and happy when they climbed out of the plane.

"Thanks for meeting us, Scott," Ethan said, surprising Dora when he embraced the other man rather than offering a traditional handshake. They were both similar height, wearing jeans and boots. But where Ethan epitomized the all-American cowboy with his wide-brim Stetson, Scott wore an Idaho State ball cap. "This is Dora and Katie," he introduced.

"Pleased to meet you." Scott wiggled his fingers at Katie. "A little girl. I never thought I'd see the day."

"Neither did I," Ethan said.

Scott raised his brows and glanced at Dora. Instead of helping Ethan out of the corner he'd obviously backed himself into, she passed Katie into his arms.

Katie experienced a moment of uncertainty, then true to her sunny disposition she adapted and immediately grabbed for Ethan's hat.

"It's a long story," he said to Scott, wrestling with Katie over possession of the hat. "Do I need to get Katie's chair thing out of the plane?"

"Car seat," Dora and Scott said in unison.

"Same thing."

"Actually, it's not," Scott corrected. "Being in the business, I can tell you there are an extensive variety of 'chair things.'"

"Then you're about to become a very happy man. I'm prepared to do some major damage to my credit card. Do I need the seat or not?"

"Not. I've got Jeremy's in the wagon. And about that credit card. You know Shelly's going to object." Scott led the way to the old white station wagon. "She doesn't charge retail to family."

"I'm a persuasive man. We'll overcome her objections."

"I'll be adding my own objections, Ethan," he said quietly, stopping to look Ethan right in the eye, his gaze moving slowly between Katie's features and Ethan's. "I owe you."

"Cut it out and let's get this show on the road."

Dora wanted to know what the undercurrents were here. There was a genuine fondness between the men, and Scott had called them family. The layers of Ethan Callahan were getting deeper by the minute. She wondered if anyone really knew this man.

And she told herself her own desire to know him was strictly for Katie's benefit.

Chapter Five

"What did Scott mean when he said he owed you?" Dora couldn't believe they'd gotten all this stuff in the airplane. Back at the ranch, they were wading amidst boxes and bags.

True to his word, Ethan had indeed spent a small fortune. And as much as she admired the pretty things, it also worried her that he'd gone to such extremes.

She didn't want him to settle in for the long haul. She only expected that she and Katie would be temporary here. The hand-carved crib, clothes, diapers, toys and accessories indicated otherwise.

To beat back the panic, she reminded herself that Ethan simply didn't do anything in half measures. When it was time to leave, she wouldn't be doing so with empty arms. By then he'd be convinced that being a father was way too limiting for his lifestyle.

"He doesn't owe me."

"Perhaps you feel that way, but he and Shelly seem to think otherwise."

Ethan shrugged, uncomfortable. "Scott's a genius

with wood. Just look at this crib. He makes them—all of them. I saw his talent and helped him get started in business.''

''He called you family?''

''We're not really.'' He gazed down at Katie, lost in thought. That part of his life held so much ugliness that he hated to remember, much less talk about it.

''I know you're adopted,'' she said. ''If you'd rather not talk about it, I understand.''

He glanced at her. He rarely thought of Fred Callahan as an adoptive father. To him Fred was his parent, first, last and always. And suddenly the pain of missing him was keen.

''How is it you know so much about me?''

''I don't know that much. Just bits and pieces of what Ozzie told my dad.''

''The curse of a small town.''

''Or a blessing. These people love you.''

And that was something he would never forget. He sighed and picked up the boxes, stacking the rest of their purchases neatly in the corner so no one would trip. ''Let's finish this in the morning,'' he said softly so as not to wake the baby.

She nodded and followed him out of the room when he switched off the light. Grant and Clay were watching a sitcom, so Ethan bypassed the entertainment room and went into the kitchen, all the while highly attuned to the small woman walking beside him. She was such an enigma, all sass and self-confidence and contradiction. She had the savvy worldly teachings of her grandparents and the moral, spiritual, simple teachings of her parents. The two made for a very special blend. She appeared to know exactly who she was and where she was going.

She was a people person, a toucher, a whirlwind who left him breathless. Two minutes after he'd introduced her to Scott and Shelly she'd acted as if they'd been best friends for years, fussing over Shelly's pregnancy and cooing over their other two small boys. She'd talked babies and retail with Shelly and woodworking and marketing with Scott. And her interest was absolutely genuine.

Yet despite her actions and her looks, there was still an innocence about her. An innocence that scared him right down to his bones.

She made him yearn when he'd had no idea he was actually yearning.

With a practiced eye he glanced around the gleaming kitchen, folded a dish towel and put it away in the drawer before opening the refrigerator.

"Want a beer?" He stopped, mentally slapped a palm to his head. "Dumb question. Let's see, there's lemonade and juice."

"I wish you'd stop doing that."

"What?"

"Treating me like a preacher's daughter."

"Well, if the shoe fits, darlin'…"

"Even if it does, I'm Dora Watkins. Just me. A woman like anybody else."

He begged to differ, but kept silent.

"And I've nothing against alcohol except that I don't like the taste. Especially beer. So I'll pass solely on the recommendation of my taste buds and opt for hot tea. I'll make it," she added when he grabbed the teakettle and began filling it with water.

"No, you sit. I think I can handle it."

She shrugged and did as he asked, for which he was fairly grateful. The woman could make a mess boiling water. It made him cringe just to watch her pouring juice in a bottle for Katie—a sticky ring left on the counter from the cap, a dribble of juice here, a splash of water there. And the concept of using a dishrag to tidy up appeared to simply escape her.

With the tea bag steeping in a cup of water, he brought it and his beer to the table and sat, leaving only the light on over the stove for illumination. A soft breeze blew the curtains, bringing with it the sound of horses settling and the noisy, three-phase song of a mockingbird. It was times like this, when the day of hard work was done and the land was quiet, that he felt a keen sense of accomplishment, of peace. Normally.

Granted, it had been a day of hard work—just not the kind he was used to. Traveling and shopping with a baby was enough to wear out even the strongest of men. As for peace, Dora and Katie had pretty much shattered that.

Funny thing, though, he couldn't seem to work up enough steam to mind. Must be the tiredness.

"My brothers and I lived on the Treechman's farm for a while," he blurted out, as though there hadn't been a lull in their conversation. "Scott was a little boy, but age didn't mean much to Bernie Treechman. If you could put one foot in front of the other and lift a stick, you were old enough and capable enough to work.''

''They were your foster family?''

''Mmm,'' he murmured, watching as she set the soggy tea bag on a napkin. Before the wetness could seep to the edges of the paper, he scooped it up and deposited it in the trash.

''Thank you,'' Dora said absently.

''Welcome.'' He sat again and stretched his legs under the table, crossed his ankles and took a sip of beer. It was an indolent pose, but his insides were anything but relaxed. ''Clay was five, Grant was six, and I was eight when our mom dropped us off at County Services in Idaho. We'd been traveling from Chicago with a boyfriend of hers. I don't even know where we were headed. I just remember that they fought the whole way, then one morning we were ushered into a building, put in a room with hard chairs and sat there holding hands quietly for an hour while our mom gave us away like stray mutts.''

''Oh, Ethan.'' Her hand streaked out to cover his. ''How awful for you.''

He automatically pulled back, not wanting her pity. Then he realized that Dora's pity—for the children he and his brothers had been and for the situation— didn't diminish him in any way.

''Yeah, it was pretty heinous. The social worker's name was Mrs. Lovell. I still remember her. She had short red hair with a wide streak of gray that swooped over her forehead like the curl on the top of a soft ice cream cone. And she had a kind voice. I begged her to let me take care of the boys, told her I was plenty old enough.'' An owl screeched, sending a chill down his spine. ''She just cupped my face and gave it a gentle squeeze. Her hand smelled like ketchup. Weird that I remember that.''

''Not really. With trauma, people usually either block it or remember it in vivid detail.''

''Sometimes I wish I could block it, but I guess I'm destined to be a detail man.'' He ran his finger down the condensation on the beer bottle. ''Mrs. Lovell wore huge glasses, the kind in the plastic frames that were too big for her face, but I could still see her eyes, the compassion and the pity. And the excitement when she came to us a couple days later and told us about the Treechmans and the ranch they ran outside of town. She said they wanted to take all of us. Together. I hugged her. God, I was scared, but she told me it would be so great because they had horses and lots of room for little boys to roam.''

Ignoring his signals for distance, Dora abandoned her tea and scooted her chair closer. He drew his legs in, but her knees still bumped his, making it hard to concentrate. Especially with the earnest expression on her face and the crisp, wildflower smell of her perfume.

She placed both her palms on his thighs and he swallowed hard.

''You weren't allowed to roam, though, were you?'' she asked softly.

He tried not to think of her touch and focused instead on the story. ''No. The Treechmans didn't want three little boys to add to their family. They wanted free labor. At first I told Grant and Clay to keep an open mind, to hope for the best. Ranching was hard work and long hours and naturally required the whole family to pitch in. But this was different. We were treated worse than dogs in the kennel.''

"But Clay was only five!" Appalled, she shook her head, her blond hair swishing across her shoulder. "And you and Grant were six and eight. That's horrible.''

"That was life.''

"No," she said resolutely. "It was not. What about Scott? Was he an only child?''

"Yes, thank God. He was Grant's age, but he looked a lot younger. He was sick a lot. So they didn't make him do the physical work, but old man Treechman had a mean tongue in his head and he used it on the kid at every opportunity.''

"How long were you there?''

"Almost a year.''

"What about Social Services? Mrs. Lovell? Didn't she come out and check on you?''

"Sure.''

"And you didn't say anything?''

He shook his head.

"Why not?''

"She'd have taken us back, and the chances of us staying together weren't good.''

"Oh, Ethan, listening to this story just makes my heart break, but at the same time I want to know the whole thing.''

"Why?''

"I don't know. I just do. So go on.''

He smiled at her fierce expression, her unapologetic

curiosity. If it had been anyone else, he would have changed the subject. For some reason talking to Dora was like confession—cleansing.

He ran his hand down his face. How could he think up an analogy like that when his body was practically humming from the touch of her warm palms on his thighs?

He scooted back in his chair, chugged a swallow of beer. "I tried to help Clay and Grant with their chores as much as possible, but it wasn't always easy because Treechman would separate us. Then one day Fred Callahan showed up to buy horses. And he bought us, too."

"He...?"

Ethan nodded. "Bought us."

"Oh. Well...how wonderful. And how scary."

"It was. Fred Callahan was a giant of a man, both in stature and in heart. He was firm but kind and filled with love. He fought for us and enlisted the help of the whole town in order to adopt us. He gave us his name and taught us all about horses and family and love."

"What a wonderful man. You must miss him."

"Very much."

"What about his wife?"

"He never married."

"Never?"

"Nope. Was a bachelor all his life and perfectly happy that way."

"Ah, so that's where you get your carefree ways."

"He was the one man I admired above all others. If I could be just a fraction of the man he was, I'd be happy. So now I guess you know more about me than almost anybody else does.''

"I appreciate you telling me.''

"I thought you should know why accepting Katie came so easily to me. With my background I'd never turn my back on a child. Dad would come right up out of his grave and get me if I did.''

"Is it just duty, then? Your acceptance of Katie?'' she asked.

"No. Maybe in the first five minutes or so. But not now. I look at that little girl, and I'm awed that she actually came from a part of me.''

Dora's hopes plummeted when he said touching things like that. As much as she admired his honor and genuine sense of responsibility, she could feel her own dreams slipping through her fingers.

"But what about a family life?''

"You mean marriage?'' He shook his head. "Not interested. My mom was married three times and lived with several others before she finally dumped us. Not a great recommendation for the institution if you ask me.''

"Ethan, it's not always like that.''

"You got a written guarantee to back that up?''

"Faith,'' she said immediately. "Love. What about the need for two parents to bring up Katie?'' Never mind that she herself would be a single parent if she were to keep Katie. At least for a time.

"We had a great family life with just Dad and us boys. Being raised in a single-parent home didn't hurt me any. I think I turned out okay. No reason why Katie won't, too.''

"But little girls need a woman's influence... especially at certain times in their lives."

"What, you think a dad doesn't know about periods and female stuff?"

"Not as well as a woman."

"Now you're being sexist. Shame on you. I happen to know men can raise girls just as well as they can raise boys. My neighbor Stony Stratton is a prime example. He's been raising his goddaughter, Nikki, since she was just a baby."

"Still—"

He put his hand over hers. "I know what you're doing, Dora."

"You do?" Was she that transparent? She didn't want to push him into making a snap decision. The wrong decision. There was nothing keeping her here other than her own declaration that she'd put him on a sort of month's probation. She didn't have any rights. Not legal ones. She'd bulldozed her way in and was only here by Ethan's good grace, manners and his admitted terror and ignorance of how to take care of a baby. That could all change in a day.

And a day was way too soon.

A lifetime was way too soon.

"Yes. You're fulfilling your promise to Amanda. And I fully understand you wanting to make sure I have Katie's best interests at heart before you leave. I can't tell you how much I appreciate you taking the time to coach us. Parents don't usually have the luxury of hands-on instructions. They just have to jump right in and get a baptism by fire."

Before you leave. Dora stood and went to the

kitchen window, absently watching the breeze flutter the open lacy curtains. She hadn't been Katie's parent, but she'd been there from the beginning, had certainly experienced the baptism by fire Ethan spoke about. She'd had to learn right along with Amanda all the ins and outs and dos and don'ts that came with children. Each day brought trials and triumphs and a love that grew deeper and stronger.

And now she was on the verge of having that love ripped right from her heart. She could well be less than a month away from losing the most important thing in the world to her. She could only hope and pray that didn't happen.

One of them was going to lose. She wasn't Katie's mother. She didn't come with the package.

Her only hope was that Ethan would see that a child didn't fit his lifestyle, that Dora was the logical one to raise Katie, adopt her.

If not, Dora loved Katie enough to let her go. She wouldn't deny the little girl the opportunity to have a father. And Ethan Callahan was a very good man.

The sting of tears pressed at the back of her throat, and she took a breath to hold them at bay, drinking in the earthy scent of animals and hay that drifted through the window. A full moon rode the eastern sky, bathing the outbuildings and corrals in a swath of white as though someone had turned on a huge spotlight.

Lost in thought, she jumped when a hand rested on her shoulder.

"Easy."

She hadn't heard him come up behind her. "Sorry.

I don't usually startle so easily." But was the jolt from fear or attraction? Just a simple touch and she felt the heat, the electricity.

"Did I say something to upset you?"

She turned to him, looked into his impossibly blue eyes. Katie had blue eyes. So did she, Dora thought. They could be a family. And where in the world had a thought like that come from? "No. I was just thinking about kids coming with owner's manuals and parents jumping into fires."

"Sounds painful."

"Can be. I'd suggest you rest up. Your marathon cram session starts tomorrow."

"Ah, I see you don't think I'm up to the task."

When he gave her that sexy grin, he was so hard to resist. "Little babies have been known to make grown men cry."

"I don't doubt it. But I happen to have a way with the ladies." His fingers toyed with the ends of her hair, coming awfully close to the swell of her breasts.

Her breath stopped in midinhalation and she had to make a conscious effort to breathe.

His gaze seemed to see all: it went from her eyes to her mouth to her chest, then back.

"I've got no business even thinking about kissing you," he murmured.

It was as though he was talking to himself rather than her. And for some reason it sparked a challenge in Dora. Maybe it was the thrill of the dare, or maybe it was simply hormones, but suddenly it became the most important thing in the world to feel his lips against hers, right here in the kitchen with the breeze blowing through the window and the peaceful sound of resting ranch animals and the not-so-peaceful yip of coyotes in the distance.

Raising up on tiptoe, she wrapped her arms around his neck and made the decision for him. "Then don't think."

She wasn't by any means a seductress, didn't have the experience for it. But Dora didn't need experience to respond to Ethan Callahan. One taste of his lips and she was lost.

Although she'd initiated the kiss, Ethan easily took over. And that's when Dora realized she might well be in over her head. She'd expected the expertise, the clever mix of gentle seduction and heat. She hadn't expected the burst of passion and sweet taste of vulnerability—whether it was hers or his, she couldn't tell.

In a movement so swift it left her reeling, his palms skimmed her rib cage, her shoulder blades, the sensitive base of her neck. With his fingers threaded through her hair, he cupped the back of her head, and Dora's entire body went boneless, her mind blank. She let him take what he needed, and she gave willingly, without the reservations and caution she'd always exercised.

She didn't need instructions for this. She played it by feel, kissed him back—for the little boy who'd been abandoned, for the man who'd lost his father, for the cowboy who didn't believe in conjugal love. And then she kissed him just for the man himself.

And for the emerging woman in her.

She surprised herself with the passion that erupted

like a crimson spray of lava. Colors burst behind her closed eyelids. She wanted more. She forgot where she was. There was only heat and desire. A desire that bordered on pain.

She moaned, then actually whimpered when he suddenly went still. Reality came crashing back with the force of an icy bucket of water.

She drew back, looked into his troubled, stunned eyes, could already see the regret, the self-castigation over getting carried away.

"Well. That was…uh, very nice."

"Dora—"

She pressed her fingers over his lips. "Don't say it." She could hardly get the words out for lack of oxygen. She'd given it all up in the kiss. "Call me Dora, or call me legs, but don't start in again with that preacher's daughter stuff."

"That's asking a lot."

"Oh, for Heaven's sake, Ethan. Get over it. It was only a kiss."

She nearly laughed when his brows shot up in affront, but she was too annoyed and off balance to expend the effort.

One kiss and her world had just turned upside down.

She wanted Katie. Desperately.

And she wanted Ethan, too.

She knew she was being greedy. But there it was.

Against all odds, crazily, she'd fallen in love. Tumbled headlong in her impulsive, never-look-back-or-ahead style. That hadn't been part of the plan, and she wasn't sure how she felt about it. Emotions, fantasies and what-ifs tripped through her mind at full speed, bringing elation and terror, giddiness and uncertainty.

Now more than ever she needed to step back, to turn over the day-to-day handling of the baby to him. If he realized caring for a child was too much to do on his own, perhaps he'd see the merits of taking on a partner.

The kind of partner he could love, honor and cherish as long as they both should live.

And she had less than a month to see how it would all play out, to see if she could accomplish this huge goal, this *shifted* goal.

Impossibly, the stakes were even higher now. If she failed, not only would her heart break from losing Katie, it would shatter from walking away from Ethan, too.

Striving to be casual, when her insides were actually a mass of nerves and arousal, she glanced at the kitchen door, gauging the steps it would take to get to the stairs and to her bedroom, to sanctuary, telling herself she would *not* run.

Once in the privacy of her bedroom she would berate herself for the foolishness of falling in love with this playboy cowboy who might never be persuaded to believe in married love.

She stepped away from him. ''Better get some sleep, hotshot. Your trial by fire starts around 6 a.m.''

Chapter Six

Ethan had scoffed at Dora's "trial by fire" taunt. By midmorning he wasn't feeling so smug. Trial by fire? This was more like Armageddon. Every man for himself. Survival of the fittest.

And he was fast learning that *he* was not the fittest.

Hardly knowing what had hit him, he found his testosterone-filled, all-bachelor ranch suddenly taken over by one small baby and a maddeningly sexy woman who he ached to touch but knew he couldn't. At least he couldn't *repeat* the touching—never mind that she'd been the one to start that gut-twisting, mind-blowing kiss. She ought to know better. And so should he.

And true to her word, she'd flitted right out of the house that morning, leaving him to blunder his way through Kid 101 all by himself. Oh, sure, she'd popped back in on him now and again—to gloat, he was certain.

Well, he wasn't a man to give up this easily.

Katie whimpered and patted at her diaper.

"Again? I just changed you." He swung the little

girl up in his arms and headed back upstairs to the yellow nursery that had taken him half the morning to get organized because as fast as he put something away, Katie crawled over and undid it. But as much as she made extra work for him, he didn't have the heart to corral her in the crib or playpen. "Seems to me if you know enough to pat your diapers this way, you ought to be ready to use a toilet."

Katie gurgled and kicked her legs as though he wasn't moving fast enough to suit her, then babbled something he had no hope of understanding. He'd figured out earlier this morning that everybody stayed happier and saner if he kept up a one-sided conversation.

"Right. You can't walk, so that's a problem. Well, we'll teach you soon enough." He laid her on the changing table, reached to get a diaper and almost let her pitch right off the tabletop.

"Whoa! What are you trying to do, give your old man a heart attack?" With one hand on Katie's belly, he tried to stretch his arm across to reach the diapers. It didn't work.

Cursing, then apologizing, he picked her up, walked the two steps to the box of disposables, then retraced his steps. He was sweating worse than he did when mucking out stalls—and imagining he could *smell* those stalls, too.

"Nothing better than a baby and a church woman to make a man clean up his language, huh, Katie?" He got the diaper off, took one look at the mess and whipped his bandanna up over his nose. "Oh, man."

"Ga-ga," Katie said helpfully.

"You got that right, sugar. No, wait! Don't move. Not the feet…oh, man," he repeated, barely suppressing the apt curse that sprang to mind.

A burst of feminine laughter from the doorway had him whipping around, glaring. Undaunted by his fierce look, Dora raised her camera and snapped a picture.

The distraction was all Katie needed. Doing a credible impersonation of a miniature greased pig she twisted right out of the smeared diaper and got up to her knees. Ethan grabbed for her and, like an expert acrobat, she used his arms as leverage to stand. In less than two seconds, she was face-to-face with him, and had his bandanna jerked off his nose, staring him straight in the eyes, bouncing like a monkey and grinning like a loon.

She was a mess. He was a mess. And despite the fiasco—as well as having his ineptness witnessed firsthand—he roared with laughter, glancing at Dora as he did so. Her camera shutter clicked once more, then lowered slowly.

Her smile was soft…different.

It caused his heart to thump against his ribs. He didn't understand the shift, the jolt to his system.

"Looks like the two of you are still surviving."

It was that gurgle of laughter in Dora's voice that had him believing he'd only imagined the odd undertones he'd thought permeated the room only seconds ago.

"Barely. For a girl, this kid does an awful lot of unladylike things."

"Now, Ethan, there's nothing unladylike about a poopy diaper."

He lifted a brow and the baby at the same time, holding her under her arms and straight out in front of him. "Are we looking at the same baby here?"

Dora laughed. "A bath will set things to rights and have her sweet-smelling in no time."

He saw her take a step back, and he took an automatic step forward, Katie still dangling out in front of him like a doll. It didn't take an expert at reading body language to tell that Dora was about to abandon him. Again.

And though he'd never been a man to beg, he wasn't above learning the art. Very quickly. But very carefully. He wasn't ready to hoist the white flag all the way just yet.

"If you could get the bath started for me, I'll grab a towel. On second thought, maybe you could get the towel, too? My hands are kind of tied up." He figured if he started in the middle of the conversation, casually, as though an agreement had already been reached, she'd act rather than think and help him out.

He was wrong.

"Actually, I just came in to get another roll of film. The guys are going to introduce me to the teasing rail—you know, where the horses flirt with one another?"

His brows slammed down. The guys—his brothers, no doubt—had no business showing her that kind of stuff. She'd likely start asking questions in that guileless way of hers, and invariably the subject would segue into sex. What in the world could Grant and Clay be thinking? "I know what the teasing rail is."

"Of course you do. But it's all new to me. And the possibilities are wonderful. Can't you just picture a greeting card with two beautiful horses nuzzling each another? It could be one of those really touching ones for lovers—apt, don't you think, since it's a teasing rail and all—"

"Dora?"

"Or I could even do a caricature sketch for laughs—"

"Dora?"

"Yes?"

Katie, smeared and smelly, still dangled happily in front of him. "Please?"

Darn her hide, she grinned.

"Baptism by fire, remember, Ethan?"

He shook his head. "I'm going to regret I ever said that."

"Losing your touch with the ladies?"

"Cute."

"Chin up, hotshot." She backed out of the doorway. "It's just a bath. You did it this morning."

"She wasn't the color of mud this morning."

"Just pretend you're hosing out one of the stalls."

"Hosing…" That gave him an idea. A little dexterity and a hand-held showerhead ought to do the job. "Fine." He waved her away. "Go play. Katie and I will survive."

His about-face seemed to make her hesitate. He wasn't going to admit defeat so early in the day.

As though she'd read his mind, her smile tipped up again. "Make sure you check the water temperature."

Shifting Katie under his arm like a sack of grain, being careful to keep the bottom half of her dangling and not touching anything, he gave Dora a direct look.

A manly, sexy, *capable* look. She was having too much fun at his expense, and it was time to take back control.

Her eyes widened, and her body went still. He allowed the moment to spin out, to wrap around them, to make absolutely certain he had her full, undivided attention.

And he accomplished just that with the single intensity of a long, provocative look.

"I know a thing or two about temperatures, legs. It's all about heat—warm heat, the slow-building kind that wraps you in a cocoon of security, innocence even," he stressed softly, deliberately. "Or fiery heat, edgy and hot like an inferno. Icy heat…" He paused, his voice dropping an octave all by itself. "Now there's an oxymoron. Ever felt icy heat, legs?"

She shook her head—an automatic, guileless gesture that told him much more than any words.

Now they were on a more even footing, and his ego took a healthy and much-needed leap. He wasn't a man used to being on the inept edge of the scale. He was used to control, to seduction, to calling the shots on the mere strength of his charm.

"Icy heat," he continued, still holding her with his eyes alone. "The kind that sends chills of pleasure up the spine. Sure you don't want to come test the water yourself?''

His question was couched in innuendo, deliberately intended to evoke images that had nothing to do with bathwater and babies. It was an adult question, a man-to-woman question. Never mind that the woman in question was the last one he should be taunting this way.

Her hands went to her camera, which hung at chest level. His gaze dropped to her breasts.

He ought to be ashamed of himself for purposefully coming on to a preacher's daughter, but the little minx was far too smug. At every turn she outwitted him, and darned if it didn't make him feel competitive. And aroused.

Ethan had enough self-control not to act on that arousal, but he liked the game, nonetheless. His smile inched up and he could feel the dimple in his cheek crease.

But the thing about smugness was that it often boomeranged right back in a person's face. At least his own did.

Dora, in all her appearance of innocence, was a master at having the last word and coming out on top. Or perhaps it was *because* of her innocence that she was able to dismiss the subject so easily, to suddenly appear so unaffected, to make him doubt his powers of seduction and his own eyesight even.

She stepped forward, gave Katie a smacking kiss on her cheek and Ethan a sassy pat on his.

''I'll pass, thanks. And opt for the warm heat, hot-shot. It's better for the baby.''

"OKAY," ETHAN SAID as he carried Katie back downstairs a good while later. Both of them had on a clean change of clothes. At least he did. Katie only wore a fresh diaper. At the rate she made messes, he didn't see any sense in continually wrestling with buttons and snaps. His bright idea of hosing her off had ended up including himself and half the bathroom, as well.

"That wasn't too bad, was it?" he asked rhetorically. "And it used up another hour. Before long it'll be lunchtime." He'd never known a day could be filled with so much activity and new endeavors and still drag so. "I don't like to go so far as to say you're boring, kiddo, but this is tough, you know? I'm used to hanging out with people who aren't quite so short—no offense—and people who talk."

Katie ignored his monologue, bent double and nearly slipped out of his arms when she spied Max. The dog didn't help matters by happily licking at the baby's bare toes, eliciting a giggle and a renewed attempt to flip out of his hold.

"Max, quit it. Why don't we all go in and watch a nice civilized cartoon? Surely the satellite dish'll pick up *Daffy Duck* or something?"

"Uck," Katie tried to parrot.

"Very good. Duck. Can you say duck?"

Instead of picking up the lesson, she wiggled to get down. Just as well. He felt like an idiot. If anybody came in here and heard him repeating words in singsong baby talk, they'd rib him clear into next year.

He set Katie on the floor and admonished Max to guard her while he flipped through the channels on the theater-size television. His fingers paused over the remote when the sports channel appeared on screen. Complements of excellent surround-sound, the room came alive with the buzzing whiz and zoom of NASCAR's finest champions, the amplified vibrations reverberating through minuscule speakers with massive power. The *vroom, vroom, vroom* of screaming engines was so true to life he could practically feel the rumble in his chest, smell and taste the rubber and spent gas.

It was too early for a beer, but it wouldn't hurt to sit and watch for a while. He didn't normally have the luxury of taking in a race in the middle of the day. Halfway to a comfortable spot on the couch, he was jerked back to reality when Katie squealed and pulled herself up on the table, snatching the magazine closest to her and ripping a page before he could juggle the remote and get to her.

"Okay, okay. I hear you. Cartoons." He hooked an arm around her soft, bare belly and lifted her to his knee, taking one last moment to appreciate Petty's skill on the inside turn before flipping the channels.

He spared an accusing glance at the dog. "Fine baby-sitter you turn out to be, Max. She was ripping magazines on your watch, you know."

Katie tried to get down. He bounced his knee, and that distracted her for all of two seconds before she did her sliding snake impersonation. Faced with the choice of catching her around the neck or letting her go, he chose the latter, and impressed himself with his ability to flip channels and move objects out of Katie's lightning-quick reach at the same time.

"Perfect," he said when the satellite finally picked up a cartoon channel. "*Dennis the Menace.* The two of you will have plenty in common, so watch."

As though absolutely mesmerized, Katie plopped right down on her diapered butt and stared raptly at the television images, her little hands with their pudgy rolls of fat creasing her wrists resting on her equally pudgy legs.

"Amazing." Ethan breathed a sigh of relief and congratulated himself on an accomplishment. He glanced at the clock in the corner. Another five minutes had passed. That was good. It was five minutes closer to lunchtime. And after that was nap time. There were schedules to follow here.

When a stallion brayed outside, Ethan was drawn to the window, the remote still in his hand. Duke of Earl was at the teasing rail with Southern Belle. With an expert eye, Ethan watched the horse's mannerisms. Duke's upper lip curled as his magnificent head lifted, a good indication that Belle was in heat. Duke called to her again, and Belle answered by laying back her ears and raising her tail.

Ethan nodded. "Okay, guys, she's ripe. Get her while she's hot."

Behind him, Katie babbled to Max. He glanced at the two of them and was sidetracked from the breeding outside. "Nice, Katie," he admonished. "Be nice to Max. He's not used to having his ears pulled."

Katie shrieked and clapped and ignored him. Thankfully the dog took the roughhousing like a docile lamb. If there had been any question in Ethan's mind over Katie's safety around Max, he would never have allowed the two in the same room together.

"Ax," she squealed, a bubble of saliva popping at her lips.

Ethan smiled. Cute kid. Messy kid, he noted as drool dribbled on her pooched-out belly. "Yeah, Max," he repeated. "Now watch the show. There's a good girl."

He looked back out the window, wishing he was out there to help his brothers. He loved being part of the process when excellent bloodlines were about to be mixed. Breeding was business, but it was also erotic, exciting, rewarding.

He glanced over to see that Katie had crawled on top of Max and was now lying out flat on the dog, slobbering on Max's yellow fur. He stepped away from the window, then stopped. Max seemed perfectly happy to allow himself to be used as a human body pillow. Katie's soft little cheek lay against the golden retriever's neck, her pudgy fingers curled just beneath the dog's ears. Maybe nap time would come before lunchtime.

"We need Dora's camera."

Katie's head sprang up, her round blue eyes sparkling. Startled, Max's head jerked up, too, his annoyed brown eyes directed at Ethan for disturbing the peace. As if anything around this baby could be remotely described as peace.

"Dody," Katie said, making a hash out of Dora's name.

"No. She's outside." Where he'd like to be, he thought.

Katie looked at the door. So did the dog. Katie patted Max—a little too hard—then plopped back down as though she'd had an exhausting day and staying up on all fours was just too taxing. Max flopped back down, too.

Ethan considered joining them both on the floor, perhaps encouraging that early nap—never mind the schedule—but the sound of breeding activity once more drew his attention to the corrals, and he moved back to the window.

He frowned when he saw Dora standing by the fence talking to Manny, one of the handlers. Just now, though, Manny wasn't doing much *handling*. He was practically falling all over himself entertaining Dora, and by the gesturing of his hands, he was obviously explaining what had transpired at the teasing rail and the next step of the process as the horses were being led around to each another, positioned and ready for Duke to cover Belle.

When he had a chance to really think about it, he decided that this wasn't necessarily the proper sight for Dora to witness. Granted, her sensibilities didn't appear to be delicate, but it was the principle of the matter—of who she was.

He might have spent a few minutes on the hypocritical line of this thinking and his own accountability for the earlier scene he'd initiated in Katie's bedroom with Dora, but Katie was on the move again, and Ethan had to abandon the window to chase after her.

She wanted up in his arms and then down. She wanted the magazines and everything else that wasn't nailed down. As fast as he cleaned up a mess, she made another one.

He heard the familiar sounds of the ranch and knew his brothers would be coming in for lunch soon. Thank God. Reprieve, for surely Dora would lend a hand with Katie.

And adult conversation. He couldn't remember when he'd last looked forward to something as simple as conversation. Words. Whole sentences that didn't just come from him. He would find out all the details of the morning, ask if the farrier had seen to Pride of Knight's shoes....

Max barked in alarm and Ethan whipped around, immediately reacting to the retriever's frenzied pitch, his heart thundering in his chest before he'd even located the source of discord. He'd only turned his back for two seconds. What now?

Katie was across the room, standing with the aid of the oak shelves to steady her, one of the knobs off the stereo unit held like a prize in her hand, her little white teeth gleaming in gleeful pride.

The destruction of his expensive entertainment equipment never even crossed his mind.

Hazards and horrors did.

Before he could get to her, she had the knob shoved in her mouth.

"No!"

Startled, she plopped on her butt and sucked in a breath.

And that was the last sound she made.

OhGodohGodohGod.

Ethan snatched her up. "Come on, baby. Don't

choke on me." He reached in her mouth, couldn't feel the disk, and that's when the fear really slammed into him. His hands trembled and he wanted to cry, wished Katie would cry.

But she was silent. Staring at him with wide, frightened blue eyes. Expecting him to do something. He was the adult. He was responsible. He was supposed to take care of her.

Yet all he could think about was panic.

Pleasepleaseplease. His heart pounded and his stomach roiled like a cauldron of acid. He flipped her around, his arm across her tummy, and had an insane thought to run. He had to get to Dora. Dora would know what to do. He was inept. A failure. He hadn't done his job right. It wasn't even noon, for God's sake, and he'd screwed up.

Fear was like a wild beast clawing at his belly as his baby daughter started to go limp. Her breathing was obstructed. She couldn't get air in or out.

He was losing her.

God, no. Please, no. Not before he'd even had a chance to have her, to know her, to see her grow and flourish, to see if her wisps of blond hair would deepen to his darker brown, to put her on her first pony and lead her around the corral.

His mouth was bone dry, and the air burned his lungs as he tried to suck it in.

"Come on, baby. Come on. Spit it out for Daddy. Please!" His heart felt as if it would pound out of his chest, but he had to focus, had to think.

Instincts took over then. For a moment he flashed on an image of the dirty alleyways of Chicago, on the helpless feelings of a little boy who had to be strong, independent…capable. A little boy responsible for the lives and safety of loved ones.

He shook away the dark images, tipped Katie forward across his forearm, prayed like he'd never prayed before.

Like a gift from above, the rough depression of his arm across her belly forced air out of her lungs and the knob shot out, bringing with it a cough and a piercing wail from Katie.

It was the most welcome sound he'd ever heard.

Hugging her to him, he sat right down in the middle of the floor and tried like the devil to get his spit back. He rubbed her back and soothed, speaking nonsense, barely aware that he'd picked up the knob and clutched it in his fist.

Katie continued to cry, and he continued to hold. Just held on tight. He wasn't cut out for this. He couldn't take it.

He was aware of voices as Dora and his brothers came in for lunch. But he never budged.

And that's how they found him, sitting on the floor, with Max whining and Katie whimpering and Ethan as still as stone, his eyes squeezed shut, just holding on.

Laughter turned to silence, then concern. Footsteps whispered like noiseless, urgent catechisms of alarm—*Can you speak? Who's hurt? What happened? What? What? What?*—as they traversed the length of the room, but Ethan didn't open his eyes.

"Ethan?"

Dora's voice. Soft and calm yet frightened. He still

didn't have the strength to look up. He needed another minute. Because just then he wasn't certain he wasn't going to join Katie in her crying jag.

"Ethan, what's wrong?"

He took a deep breath, ran his palm softly over Katie's back, rubbed his chin over her silky, nearly nonexistent hair.

Dora's perfume swirled around him as she dropped to her knees beside him, placed one of her hands on his back, the other over his on Katie's back. "Ethan, talk to me, please. You're scaring me."

"You'll have to stand in line." He cleared his throat. "I'm scared enough for ten people right now." He glanced up at Grant and Clay, who were also hovering. His look was accusing, even when he knew darn well the incident wasn't their fault. It was nobody's fault but his own for taking his eyes off Katie. Still, he opened his palm, showing the knob.

"Damn," Grant breathed, and didn't even apologize for the language. He knelt down. "She got it in her mouth?"

"Yeah, and nearly choked."

"Is she okay?" Clay asked.

"Better than me," Ethan said, because Katie was now thoroughly intrigued by the small huddle they were all in—and she was the center of attention. Even Max had nosed his way back into the circle.

"Ax," Katie whispered, and Ethan pressed his lips against her sweaty temple.

"Max barked to warn me," Ethan told his brothers and Dora, unable to get the horror out of his mind. He'd been stomped by an unruly stallion, seen men gored and bloodied on the ranch and in rodeos, but nothing seemed to compare.

Dora's hand was still on his back, soothing him, he realized. He glanced at her. "How do you do this?"

She seemed to understand. "Babies are quick, Ethan. Sometimes you have to wonder how they ever make it past toddler stage with the stuff they get into and do."

"Don't even say that." Katie was making noises as if she'd like to get loose, but he wasn't ready to let her go just yet. He wiped the lingering tears off her round, squishy cheeks and nearly lost his hold on his emotions when she reached up and patted his face.

"Here, why don't I take her," Dora said.

He nodded. "Thanks. I could use a few minutes to find my knees."

"I'll go see about lunch. Is your stereo ruined?"

"Screw the stereo," Ethan burst out.

"Who cares about the stereo," Grant said at the same time.

"Stereos can be replaced," Clay chimed in simultaneously.

There was a beat of silence when Ethan relived the horrible experience all over again. "Yeah, they can be replaced," he said softly. "But Katie can't."

"She's fine, Ethan." Dora put a hand on his arm, stepping closer when Katie reached out a hand to do the same. She brought them into a circle. A family circle.

The thought winged out of nowhere, startling him. "If you don't mind getting a head start on lunch, my brothers and I'll spend a few minutes in here babyproofing the room.''

Dora laughed. ''With this many sophisticated bigboy toys, it'll take more than a few minutes. And, hey, look on the bright side, Ethan. At least she didn't get swept into the wall like a James Bond stunt or something.''

''Don't joke,'' he said, then felt the blood rush from his head. ''My God, that could have happened. I was messing with the remote, looking for cartoons. I turned the sensor back on.''

Babyproofing was going to be a bigger project than he'd anticipated. Dora had needled him about his lifestyle and how a baby would fit into it.

Today he saw just how far removed his world was from that of a man with a lifetime responsibility of a child.

Chapter Seven

"Okay, sweet girl, you gotta help me out here. I'm starting to look bad. You make messes that send me into a tailspin, take my stereo knobs and nearly choke to death, and now you're about to turn me into a zombie." Ethan was exhausted, and clearly Katie was, too, but she wasn't going to bed as easily as Dora claimed she normally did.

Katie raised her arms, crying pitifully, and Ethan lifted her back out of the crib. "Okay, we'll negotiate. I'll rock, and you sleep. And you can have the pacifier if you promise not to stick it anywhere weird or swallow it whole."

Warm and cuddly, she latched on to the pink suckie thing and snuggled into his arms as he rocked, her eyelids growing heavy, then popping back open as she fought sleep harder than a bronc rider fights to stay on his mount.

Resting his head against the back of the rocker, he absently listened to the lulling creak, creak, creak of the wood and thought about the day.

After the choking incident, Ethan had wanted to

run as far away from responsibility as he could. He'd been afraid to touch lest he screw up, afraid to trust himself alone with the baby. And though Dora had spent a good part of the afternoon with him, easing him back into the routine, she'd more or less told him to get a grip, had actually used the trite, "falling off a horse and getting back on" cliché. That said, she'd gone right back on her merry way, perching a kitten in the window to sketch, snapping pictures of everything that moved, charming his brothers and his ranch hands...and him.

The woman was an intriguing mix of self-assurance, innocence, fun and perpetual motion. She could soothe with a touch, inflame with a look and wear a man out just watching her busyness.

And it was getting more difficult by the minute to remember that he was supposed to keep his hands off her.

A burst of laughter from downstairs had him tensing and looking quickly down at Katie. The creak of the rocker ceased as he went still, held his breath. She didn't stir, was thankfully asleep, undisturbed by whatever was going on below.

Carefully he stood, then froze again when she inhaled and exhaled deeply. So far so good. He laid her in the crib, covered her with a light blanket, had an urge to run his palm over her angelic cheek but was afraid even the light touch would energize her once more and he'd have to start all over with the bedtime process.

How one little baby could get the better of a strong, thirty-four-year-old man was beyond him.

Leaving the door slightly ajar, Ethan made his way downstairs, annoyed when more laughter sounded. Didn't anyone in this household realize there was a baby sleeping? Didn't they care he'd just spent a grueling half hour trying to quell heart-wrenching sobs, each involuntary snuffle etching parental scars on his soul?

Evidently not. His brothers and Dora were in a hot and heavy game of… Ethan's brows jerked together and he came to a stop just inside the room.

They were playing *poker,* of all things. And laughing like demented fools.

"Do you think this is appropriate?" he asked, wisely leaving off the, *for a preacher's daughter* part of his thought.

Dora looked at him, her pretty blue eyes sparkling, her smile wide and welcoming and just this side of mischievous. "Ethan! Come join us."

Ethan had a better understanding of how the first man in creation had buckled to temptation so easily. Dora Watkins made it difficult to remember the merits of honor, restraint and his own vows to resist.

"Gambling, legs?"

"In a manner of speaking. And I'm whipping these guys' tails." She waved a handful of matchsticks at him. "Care to see if you can change the house's luck?"

"Now, Dora," Grant said. "I wouldn't exactly say you're winning."

"No? Then who, may I ask, just finished kissing his brother on the lips?"

Clay ran a hand down his face, clearly embarrassed, and Grant shrugged, typically unconcerned.

Ethan shook his head, felt a smile tug and sat down before he could think better of it. "My brothers were kissing?"

"Truth or dare," Dora explained. "Those are the stakes. Grant lost the hand, chose dare over truth, and I called it."

"I still don't see why *I* should have been penalized," Clay griped.

"Because my full house beat your flush."

"Yeah, and I'm still flushed."

Dora grinned. "It's a becoming color. And you're such a sport. My brothers kiss all the time."

"On the lips?" Grant and Clay asked in unison. She had both men eating out of her hand, which surprised Ethan. Like him, his brothers were flirts, appreciated a pretty woman and the fine art of conversational banter. But they usually hid behind a barely discernible emotional wall, affected an unconscious distance and sexual aloofness that kept them in the driver's seat and had women's hearts going pitty-pat. Clearly, it was Grant's and Clay's hearts that were stuttering, and Dora was holding the reins.

"Not actually on the lips," she said with a little choke of laughter, "but what's a dare if you don't add a little spice?" She anted four matchsticks and expertly dealt the cards, flinging them as smoothly and quickly as a seasoned dealer in a Las Vegas casino. "Standard five-card draw," she said to Ethan. "And nobody folds since we're not playing for money."

"I think I know how to play the game, legs."

Her blond brows arched impudently. "I'm sure you do, cowboy. Guts to open."

Typical of the way his luck was running today, he didn't have a blessed thing in his hand. And his guts had taken a beating from one small little baby. "I'll bet two matchsticks," he said, shoving the red-tipped spears into the ante.

When it came back around to Dora, she matched Ethan's two and raised the pot by one more. "Cards?" she asked the table at large, looking directly at Ethan.

"I'll take four. Did you learn these gambling skills at church, too?"

"Ah-ah." She shook her head. "You're jumping the gun. It's not time for truths yet." She passed him the requested number of cards and continued around the table, the momentum of her arm actions causing her body to sway and her knee to bump his with each toss.

It was incredibly distracting, making him want to jerk her right onto his lap and initiate full-body contact rather than intermittent, teasing taps.

"Bets?"

He shoved out six matchsticks, his hand colliding with Dora's when she shifted again. He almost wondered if she did it deliberately. He considered scooting his chair over a bit, but discarded the idea. Evidently, he was into masochism today.

He was playing poker with a saint, and his thoughts were edging toward pure sin.

Her skin looked smooth, her nails short and clear

of polish. He knew what her touch felt like on his arm, both soothing and arousing, wondered what it would feel like against the rest of him.

She had her bottom lip sucked between her teeth, concentrating. That mouth was something. Quick to smile, even quicker to sass.

And it packed a powerful punch in a kiss.

"Ethan?"

His gaze jerked up. Everyone was staring at him—Dora in puzzlement, his brothers in disapproval. He ignored all of them.

"We've called your bet, now what have you got?" Dora asked.

He looked at his hand. "Not a damned thing."

Clay had a pair of twos, which was still better than Ethan's nothing. Grant smugly fanned out three of a kind, and Dora, trying to look prim and apologetic—and failing miserably—laid down a straight.

All eyes turned to Ethan.

"Truth or dare?" Dora asked, leaning in, her pert breasts brushing the table. His body reacted like lightning, muddling his thoughts.

He didn't want to kiss his brother or stand on his head, so he said, "Truth."

Since Dora had officially won the hand, Clay and Grant looked at her to see what she'd come up with.

"What's the worst thing you ever did?"

"Stole." It was out before he knew it. For what seemed like an eon, nobody in the room moved. Then Grant and Clay looked away, erecting walls, pretending they didn't all share memories that scraped them raw. Pretending they didn't know that the memories were worse for Ethan.

After only the barest pause, as though she were gleefully waiting for more juicy details and found absolutely nothing amiss, Dora flicked her hair behind her ear and defused the tense moment with a crisp shuffle of the cards.

"I stole a quarter from the collection plate once," she imparted in a mock-scandalized whisper.

Astonished, yanked right out of his self-absorbed focus, Ethan's brows shot up. "It wasn't your turn for truth."

"Oh. I keep forgetting the rules."

Like hell, he thought.

"I've never told another living soul that secret." She happily gave the cards another crisp shuffle. "Isn't it cleansing to unburden this way?"

He stared at her, wanted to kiss her so bad he actually leaned forward, forgot all about his brothers and vows and virtues. Dora Watkins was full of verve and effervescence…and an intuitiveness that was sharp and gentle and should not have surprised him as it did.

She'd understood his discomfort, thought to ease it with her own blurted declaration, to let him know it was okay, that he was human just like everyone else.

That he was worthy enough to sit at a poker table with a preacher's daughter.

Man alive she was something.

At the last moment he checked the impulse to cover that smiling mouth with his own. "Deal the cards, legs."

"Certainly...cowboy."

His lips twitched. Yep. Definitely something.

This time Dora lost the hand, and though it was actually Clay's turn to pose the truth-or-dare question because he'd won the round, Dora barreled right ahead in her whirlwind fashion.

"Truth," she announced. "I posed nude in art class."

"Dora!" all three men shouted at once.

She nearly fell out of the chair laughing.

Studying her, Ethan decided they'd been had. Odd that it was his gaze she appeared to seek out, to cling to—even though he wasn't the only man at the table. And though her obvious, deliberate intention was to shock all three of them, it was his reaction that she seemed most ghoulishly interested in. "You did not."

"I did, too."

"How could you?"

"It was art!" she defended, affronted.

"You're really telling the truth?" Ethan asked.

"Of course. We're not playing *liar's* poker."

She kept him so off balance he had trouble remembering his own name, much less what they were playing.

He scooted back his chair. "I think we should call it a night," he said, looking at his brothers, who'd lost their scandalized expressions a lot quicker than Ethan had. "I don't *even* want to know what she'd do on a dare."

Grant shrugged and casually leaned back in his chair. "*I'd* like to know. How about you, Clay? Want to take a vote?"

Clay grinned. "I'm all for it. Seems she owes us, anyway, for that kissing incident."

Ethan scowled, stood and plucked the cards out of Dora's hands. "Nobody's going to kiss anybody else. This isn't a democracy, and I'm pulling rank."

"Who said you had rank?" Grant asked, deliberately needling him, Ethan was sure.

"I did. I'm the oldest."

"Ah, in that case, old man, we'll defer to your ancientness." Grant and Clay stood. "Thanks for the game, Dora. See you in the morning."

Ethan watched his brothers saunter out of the room and he felt like an idiot. Where had all his sophistication gone? Why did he feel as though his world was spinning out of control around him? If he had any sense at all, he'd run right up those stairs and take himself to bed, too. Take himself right out of temptation's way.

Instead, he looked into the eyes of the temptress. And it was getting harder by the second to remember who she was.

"Well, you certainly know how to clear a room."

"Me? You're the one getting naked in art class!"

She burst out laughing. "You mean to tell me, I actually shocked the worldly Ethan Callahan?"

A grin tugged at his lips. The little imp. The urge to pick her up and carry her over to the sofa for a good old-fashioned session of necking was about to get the better of him.

"Yeah, you shocked me. Want a beer? Scratch that. I forgot you don't like the taste. How about a soda?'' He opened the bar refrigerator and peered inside.

''Something without caffeine'll be fine.''

''Picky, picky. Good thing you didn't ask for diet.''

''Yuck. Can't stand the taste. I'm very choosy about what I put in my mouth.''

He cracked his head on the refrigerator door. Looking at her, he realized she didn't have a clue to the erotic connotations and images her words had evoked.

Preacher's daughter, Ethan. That adds up to virgin. Which equals off-limits. Remember it.

After that little pep talk, he took a breath, grabbed the beer and soda and went to the couch.

Another miscalculation. She scooted right up next to him, smelling like sunshine and purity. When her lips touched the soda can, he was mesmerized by the tilt of her head, the slender column of her neck, the way tendrils of wheat-colored hair shifted against her shoulders and the back of the sofa.

She leaned forward and set the can on the oak coffee table, then folded her legs beneath her and settled in, turning toward him so that her knees rested against his thigh.

''You know, my curiosity is just awful. Even when something's none of my business, it still gnaws at me. Ever have that happen?''

He picked up her soda can and put a coaster beneath it. She didn't appear to notice. ''I usually try to stick to things that're my business,'' he said.

''See there. That's the difference between us.''

''There are *big* differences between us, Dora. What do you want to know? Why I stole? What I stole?''

"Yes," she said without an ounce of shame. "You don't have to tell me, of course. On the other hand—"

Old memories twisted in his gut, dark edges that made his voice sharper than he intended. "Maybe you'd like to know if I've got nasty secrets that'll make me a bad influence on Katie?"

"Oh, Ethan." Dora scooted closer, put her hand on his shoulder, ran it up his neck to toy with his hair. "That didn't even cross my mind. I'm sorry. I should never have brought it up. Sometimes I just don't think."

The feel of her fingers against his hair sent chills over his spine. He took her hand in his. "No. I'm sorry. I didn't mean to snap." Because it seemed so natural, he linked his fingers with hers and drew their joined hands down to his thigh, running his thumb over the back of her smooth, white skin.

"I told you our mom dropped us off at the County Services in Idaho. Before that, we lived in Chicago. None of us have the same fathers, or even know who they are, so there was very little stability—or money—in our lives. My mother just seemed to pop babies out, then go on her next man hunt, forgetting all about us, leaving us to fend for ourselves."

"That's horrible."

"Yes. But what we went through made Grant and Clay and me closer than most pure-breed brothers."

She found it odd that he would use that term, but didn't interrupt him.

"We were pals, had to stick together, and a lot of the time, that was on the dirty streets of Chicago."

"You didn't have a home?"

"Sometimes. We moved a lot, though. One crummy room looked about the same as the next. And the times she managed to get us in someplace halfway decent, we'd get kicked out soon enough for not paying the rent. I tried to help out, did odd jobs for the buildings' superintendents, collected bottles and cans for recycling money. But it never was enough to keep the roof over our heads or food in our bellies."

Dora squeezed his fingers tighter. Through the church, she'd come upon a lot of needy families, but never ones who'd been through such poverty and horror. Never ones whose children had been forced to act as the adults. Oh, she knew it happened, but she'd been insulated from it for the most part. Hearing Ethan's flat voice, seeing the dull light in his blue eyes as he looked inward nearly broke her heart.

"I was the oldest one, and I felt responsible. The first time I stole, it was a loaf of bread. I couldn't even eat any of it. The next time it got easier. The day a scumbag tried to offer money for Grant was when I stopped worrying about morality and concentrated on surviving. I had to protect them."

"Ethan, stop. You don't have to relive this."

He rubbed his thumb over the pulse on her wrist. "No, it never got that ugly. I didn't let it. But that was when I learned about rage. It was like a beast inside me, something nasty that scared the hell out of me. I hit the guy right where it counts with a half-full bottle of whiskey, stole his wallet when he was doubled over, then busted the bottle against his head and got the boys out of there."

"Good for you."

He turned to her, traced a finger over her cheek. "I could have killed that guy, Dora. Doesn't any of this shock you?"

"No." *Maybe.*

He studied her for a long moment. "You're so...I don't know. Accepting. Forgiving."

"Ethan, there's nothing to forgive. You were a neglected child." She wanted to put her hand over his, press a kiss on the rough skin of his palm, use her lips to worship those hands that had committed acts of lawlessness out of love and honor. His motivation was commendable in her mind.

But if she carried through on her impulse, he'd more than likely pull away from her, etch that line he seemed so determined to draw between them.

"I tried to make sure my brothers worked for their money, and I tried to do the same. But the pay for an eight-year-old wasn't enough to keep food in our stomachs. So, while the boys took over collecting recyclables out of trash bins, I moved through the streets and picked pockets." He sighed and rested his head against the back of the couch. "I wish I had names and addresses for everyone I stole from. I'd give it back."

"What about your mother?"

He shrugged, his broad shoulders pulling at the seams of his white T-shirt. He was slouched on the sofa, but the relaxed pose didn't disguise the tension.

"She was like a cat who always landed on her feet. She had plenty of men to take care of her and usually couldn't be bothered with us much. She saw that we were surviving and left us to it, never wanted to know *how* we managed. I was always a little surprised she actually took us with her when she left Chicago with the last guy. Anyway, I've pretty much told you the rest. She dumped us, then the Treechmans got us, then Dad came along.''

For a moment he seemed to draw inward, and Dora waited quietly, allowing him all the time he needed for a mental walk through his past. His eyes were closed, his chest rising and falling beneath the soft, body-hugging T-shirt that was tucked into jeans the color of an icy-blue lake.

He was a beautiful man, thrilling to look at, with long legs, lean hips and a muscular torso that inspired fantasies that were terribly inappropriate just now.

Still, she wondered if he would flinch if she laid her palm over that washboard-flat stomach, traced the raised pattern of horseshoes on his wide leather belt, leaned down to get a better look at the intricate carvings on his oversize silver buckle.

Realizing those thoughts were even more inappropriate, she raised her gaze back to his face. He had features that might have been carved by the angels, features that would make any student of art clamor to study. Dora's own fingers itched for her sketch pad and pencils.

He lifted their joined hands, drawing her closer, and Dora realized his inward images had wound down.

"I gave Dad a pretty hard time at first, but he was so filled with love and patience that the anger in me gradually went away."

But not the memories, she thought. A part of him would always wonder what he'd done to deserve such bad beginnings—or the good that had come his way, for that matter. She wished she could convince him it wasn't his fault, but if all the years with Fred Callahan hadn't been able to, she surely couldn't.

"Did you ever hear from your mom again?"

He shifted his head against the back of the couch and looked at her. "When I was seventeen a lawyer came out to the ranch with a check for an obscene amount of money. Seems good old mom finally married well…and became a rich widow. Before she could enjoy her wealth, though, she got sick, and in an attack of remorse, I guess, she willed her money to us."

"She died, then?"

"Yeah. And I didn't feel sad. And I didn't want to take a penny of her money, I didn't want the memories attached. She'd abandoned us, allowed us to live like dogs on that ranch. Grant and Clay felt the same. But Dad convinced us that the money was our due. He told us to contribute a good chunk of it to charities, to help other boys who'd suffered similar situations as ours, and then enjoy the rest. He coached us with shrewd investment advice so our nest eggs could grow—and manipulated us by telling us the amassing fortune meant all the more money we could give away to those in need."

"Which you do on a regular basis." It was a statement, not a guess.

"Yeah. It's the damnedest—uh, darnedest—thing. Everything we touch seems to turn to gold. I try to give the stuff away and it just grows back like fat, healthy weeds.''

She grinned. "Want to know which scripture that comes from?"

She'd intended for him to smile. Instead he looked even sadder.

"Darlin', haven't you been listening? I'm no saint, and I doubt the Man Upstairs is looking down on me very favorably right now. I don't know who my biological father is, and because of that I'd sworn never to subject a child to the same circumstances—but I did. Or nearly did. I'd like to think I can make it right, but am I really a good enough role model?"

"Of course you are. Forgiveness is a gift, Ethan."

"That's what Dad always said. But when the memories creep in, it's harder to remember."

She wondered what he held back, what darker hurts the young boy in him had suffered. But she wouldn't push, didn't want to know, nor did she need to know. Ethan was a good man, no matter what he said to the contrary.

It was ironic. A week ago his concern over not being good enough would have thrilled her, been the perfect opening to slide adoption papers across the negotiating table, been just the thing she would have capitalized on to gain custody of Katie.

She would have simply considered it God's will and happily gone on her way—working out a visitation agreement with him of course. She would never want to keep his child from him, or deny Katie the privilege of knowing him, and Madison wasn't all that far from Shotgun Ridge.

Now, she felt different. She hurt for him, needed to help him realize what a good, decent man he was. She couldn't bear the thought of him not keeping Katie.

And even more than that, she couldn't bear the thought of him not keeping her.

Chapter Eight

Ethan couldn't find his boots. Katie was yelling her lungs out in the bedroom—obviously having suffered no ill effects from yesterday's choking horror—and here he stood in his socks, unable to get completely dressed for the day. To heck with it.

He grabbed his hat off the marble-top dresser and frowned when he noticed tufts of fur flying. On closer inspection, he realized it was cat hair.

Dora.

Katie's cries got louder. He stepped up his pace and was in the yellow room in three strides.

"All right. No sense in all the racket, I've got decent ears." He lifted her out of the crib and nearly swore. Wet as a frog, she'd just soaked his shirt, too. Again. She immediately hushed and smiled.

Snatching up a diaper from the bottom of the box and a clean little outfit with pink bunnies on it, he headed back toward his room.

Dora was standing at the bottom of the stairs. "I've got her," he said, realizing she'd heard Katie's cries and had probably thought he'd forgotten about the kid or gone hard-of-hearing or something.

And while he was in a fine snit and she was within glaring distance, he stopped and turned the full force of his displeased gaze on her.

"Have you by any chance been photographing cats?"

"Why, yes. How did you know?"

He held out his fuzz-filled hat. "Woman, don't you know a man's hat is sacred?"

"Uh, no."

"Well it is. And speaking of sacred articles of clothing, you haven't seen my boots, have you? Brown?" he described. "Nice and soft and well broken in?"

She wouldn't meet his gaze. That didn't bode well. Dora always met his gaze head-on. Most of the time the trait was fairly disconcerting.

"Dora?"

"Um, I might have seen them...somewhere."

"Don't tell me you put the cat in there, too."

"No, of course not. The boots were for the puppies."

He didn't even bother to sigh. He had a soggy baby on his hip who'd already soaked the front of his shirt with pee and was now drenching his shoulder with slobber. He'd overslept—Dora's fault because he'd had erotic dreams about her—Katie was almost out of diapers, and today was the day the Callahans had planned to tease Warrior and Sunday Best who'd make an excellent match, though they'd previously resisted each other.

But the baby still had to be fed, he had to change, and by the time he'd accomplished all that, the fireworks were likely to be over. Plus he had to deal with cat hairs in his hat and God knows what the puppy had done in his boots.

And while he stood there with his insides ripping every direction in turmoil, Dora gazed up at him with her fresh-faced innocence; her killer body in frayed jeans shorts and breast-hugging tank top; her sun-streaked blond hair kissing her smooth shoulders and tumbling over her back.

She was the antithesis of him in every way. He was earthy, worldly and organized. She wouldn't know organized if it came up and shook her hand in formal introduction.

So what was it about her that made him want to bask in her presence? What devil was it that came to him in the middle of the night to toy with his sub-conscious and plant ridiculous thoughts in his mind, cause him to ask inappropriate questions of himself like, "Is she the one?" He didn't want anybody to be "the one."

"Well, it looks as though you've got everything under control, so I'll just leave you to it," she said, starting to back away from the stairs.

He should have kept his mouth shut. *Should have* and *did* were miles apart. "So, is your dance card full for the day?"

"Yes." Her answer was immediate and unapologetic as she glanced from him to the baby.

He knew what she was thinking—that he wanted

her to help him out with Katie. He liked being the one to surprise for once.

"That's too bad. I was planning to go into town for a while and thought you might like to join me."

"Oh. Isn't that interesting. My card just opened up."

He felt his smile form slowly, starting in his gut and growing all the way to his eyes. "God'll get you for fibbing, legs."

"I wasn't fibbing. I answered your dance card question in the spirit with which it was posed. What are we doing in town?"

"Shopping and lunch. Katie's out of diapers and I've a hankering for one of Brewer's greasy burgers."

"My kind of man. Shopping and food will get me every time."

IT TOOK NEARLY AN HOUR to get Katie dressed and fed and all the baby paraphernalia gathered. He tried putting her in the backpack he'd bought at Scott and Shirley's store, but she immediately invented a new and annoying game of knocking off his hat. After he'd retrieved it for the fourth time in as many minutes, he considered just leaving it off. But he felt naked. The sun was warm, and he just didn't feel dressed going to town without his hat.

Abandoning the backpack in favor of the stroller, he rolled her out of the house. This was a better arrangement, anyway. The stroller had a shade over the top to protect her, and he wanted to go out and check on the progress of Warrior and Sunday Best before they left. It would have to be a quick check, though, because Katie was completely out of diapers now.

"Ethan, honestly. If we're going to town, Katie ought to be dressed."

He looked at Dora, who was waiting for him outside, then down at Katie. "She's dressed."

"In her pajamas."

Pajamas? He lifted the stroller's top, peered down at the cotton gown with pink bunnies on it and shrugged, unconcerned. "She doesn't mind. Just looks like she's wearing one of those long dresses girls are so taken with these days. And since both her hair and her vocabulary is limited, the bunnies and sandals will do the talking and eliminate any accidental gender insults."

Dora smiled. "Don't count on it. I had her in a frilly pink dress with lace socks and a pink headband with a bow on it and some lady actually asked me how old *he* was."

"You're just hanging out with the wrong people. The folks in Shotgun Ridge are sharper than that. Let's take a walk over to the breeding shed for a minute. I need to check on something."

"Warrior and Sunday Best?"

"Yes."

"They've been teasing half the morning and neither one is cooperating."

He stopped. He still wasn't altogether comfortable with her witnessing some of the operations on the ranch. "How do you know?"

"I was out with the...uh, the puppies, and I stopped in to watch." She glanced away.

As well she should. She'd tripped over her words because those *puppies* had *pooped* in his boots. He started to scowl all over again and then decided it wasn't worth the energy. Dora had delivered his boots with an apology for taking them without permission. So why would anyone expect her—a woman who would more than likely walk right over the disasters left by a tornado without noticing—to look inside a pair of boots for surprises?

"So did they abandon the attempt for the day?" he asked to distract himself.

"Yes. They brought in Foolish Pride and she was much more receptive to the liaison, so they went with it."

"And you watched."

"Of course. It's quite exciting."

That gleam in her eye made him nervous and he had no idea why, so he looked away.

Buttery sunshine shone out of an endlessly blue sky where puffy white clouds rode the breeze like huge dollops of whipped cream. A perfect day to breed a champion. He should have figured they'd have trouble with Warrior and Sunday Best. For some reason, he related those two horses to Dora and himself. Perhaps it was just as well the two didn't suit. A randy warrior had no business courting a Sunday girl.

"I guess since you've given the breeding report I was after, we can go."

"Ready when you are."

Ethan loaded the stroller, the car seat and half of Katie's worldly belongings into the Cadillac, ignoring Dora's helpful suggestion that they'd likely not need *all* of the stuff. But Ethan was fast learning that it paid to be prepared for anything.

Katie napped on the way to town and woke up refreshed and happy—and wet.

"Looks like diapers are an emergency rather than a necessity now," he said, noting that her dress—or pajamas, rather—were also damp. "Am I doing something wrong with these paper things? They don't hold near enough water if you ask me."

"Let me see." She lifted Katie's gown and chuckled. "Uh, Ethan, you've got this diaper on backward."

"I do not."

She nodded again, bit her lip.

He scowled. "This is how I've always done it."

All three days. "Didn't you notice the back side was slightly larger than the front?"

"No. They looked pretty even to me. I went by the tapes. An envelope's flap is in the back. That's where the sticky stuff is."

"A diaper's not an envelope."

"Same principle. You're sealing the kid in there."

"Trust me. The flaps on the diaper stick in the front."

"Then there ought to be some arrows or something. A tag stating front and back."

"The directions are on the box."

"Like I actually have time to look at the box when she's squirming like a floppy fish. In case you've forgotten in the last three days, while you've been enjoying a fine vacation from kid duty, Katie deliberately messes up her diapers, even though she obviously can't stand the way it feels, then she lets you know immediately. And patience isn't one of her strong suits. That doesn't leave a lot of time for locating and reading instructions.''

''Doesn't it make you proud to have recognized this personality trait of your daughter's?''

''It'd make me prouder if she'd just ask to use the toilet.''

''We'll have to work on the walking before we can tackle that.''

He pounced on the ''we'' part. ''Good. Then you'll help me give walking lessons before you go?''

He had no idea what he'd said to make her sparkling eyes go all sad that way. Then he realized that it would probably be difficult for her to walk away from Katie. He started to tell her she could stay as long as she wanted, get used to the idea of having her freedom again, but she turned and looked around the town as though the weird moment had been all in his imagination.

''Why don't you meet me at Brewer's Saloon when you're done shopping,'' she said.

''You mean you're not going with me?''

She turned back to him then. ''You need to know if you can handle a shopping trip on your own.''

''I already know I can.''

''Then hop to it, and if you're real lucky, I'll buy you an ice cream to go with those greasy burgers.''

Before he could agree or disagree, or further his case for wanting company on the shopping trip, she'd started across the street toward the saloon.

He didn't worry about turning her loose on the

town when she didn't know anybody. Shotgun Ridge's main drag was barely a block long. And Dora didn't have a bit of trouble blending in and meeting folks on her own. He had an idea you could plunk her down in a mud puddle and she'd be perfectly happy. She was adaptable. Special. Fun.

Katie squirmed and whimpered, patting her diapers.

"Evidently Dora forgot to teach you that patience is a virtue?" Katie blinked and grinned. "Not to worry. We've got a preacher and Sunday school here— maybe not exactly like you're used to at Dora's daddy's church, but it's the same teachings." He moved down the sidewalk toward the general store, keeping up a one-sided conversation as though it were the most natural thing in the world.

"Your old man might have a past littered with sin, but that doesn't mean I don't intend to bring you up right. And we'll *both* read the instructions on the diaper box. I can't believe you didn't say something in the first place rather than peeing all over me and everything else."

Katie giggled, and Ethan felt he'd successfully distracted her from her wet bottom. He stepped into the cool interior of Tillis's General Store and actually felt like preening when all eyes fastened on him— predominately women's eyes.

Complements of Ozzie Peyton, Lloyd Brewer, Vernon Tillis and Henry Jenkins—more affectionately known as the geezers—the town's population of women was growing steadily. Between the advertisements they'd put in newspapers and magazines— claiming they had a bunch of bachelor cowboys and not enough women and babies—and the bachelor auction, women were showing up by the carloads.

Ethan noticed a wider variety of groceries stocking the shelves and three rows of brand-new shopping carts rather than the ten or so rickety ones that had been here since he'd first arrived twenty-six years ago. The number of carts seemed a bit excessive—this wasn't a huge supermarket with long, wide aisles. It was perhaps fifteen hundred square feet with closely spaced, short gondolas that required hairpin turns and would likely cause major pileups if too many baskets tried to navigate at once.

"Let's live a little dangerously, toots," he said to Katie and plopped her in the fold-out seat section of the cart. Her gown bunched up around her thighs. "Okay, next time you can wear pants." She patted her diapers again. "I know, I know. Your butt's wet and we're gonna fix that."

He waved to Vera Tillis and wheeled the cart around the store, even though he hadn't a clue where the baby stuff was. He'd never been down that aisle before. But zipping around tight aisles on brand-new wheels that didn't wobble appealed to his sense of adventure. Kind of like hugging tight barrels on a superbly responsive quarter horse.

"Hey, Vera," he hollered. "I need diapers."

"So I've heard. In the back, to the right." She came over to join him. "Oh, isn't she just a love. And she's the spitting image of you. Katie, is it?"

See there? The pink bunnies were a dead giveaway. He wished Dora was here to witness the automatic recognition due to her pink outfit. It was probably the short hair that caused the resemblance to him. That and the blue eyes and the grapevine. "And just how is it you know her name?"

"Ethan, you forget where you are and who my husband is!" Vera laughed. "May I?" Before he could answer, Vera had Katie lifted out of the basket.

"Careful," he said. "She's wet."

"Oh, that's all right, isn't it sweetie?" Vera said.

At last. A woman willing to help out. Well, that wasn't strictly fair. Dora had backed off for his own good, she'd said. She was making sure he learned by *doing*.

He just hadn't realize the *doing* was going to be quite this hair-raising.

Katie was perfectly happy going to Vera, which gave him a belated twinge. That wasn't good, was it? He'd have to teach her not to talk to strangers. But how did you get a kid to distinguish between a friend and a stranger? He'd think about that later.

"Okay, what is it you know, Vera?"

"That this precious little girl is your daughter. Ozzie knows your friend Dora's father, Ben Watkins. And of course when Ozzie sinks his teeth into something, he naturally shares it with Vern and the others."

"Naturally. They're thinking about matchmaking again, aren't they, Vera?" One good thing about the gossip mill—he might get some speculative looks, but it would reduce the number of times he would have to repeat himself.

And repeatedly admitting that he'd recklessly made

a baby wasn't something he relished. Never mind that Katie was a child anyone could be proud of.

Vera smiled and handed Katie a plastic teething ring to chew on. "You always were a very smart boy, Ethan."

"Yeah, well next time you see the fearsome foursome, tell them I'm on to their games. I've got more than I can handle with that little bundle right there."

How could those old guys even have thought about trying to match him up with a preacher's daughter? Where were their minds?

He loaded the basket to the brim with diaper boxes, and nearly cleaned out the shelves of the baby aisle. He paused over the single application enema that claimed to be gentle and noninvasive—if such a thing were possible—then went ahead and tossed it in the cart. You never knew when a baby might get her plumbing stopped up, though based on his recent experience, Katie didn't have any problems in that area.

The diaper change presented a bit of a problem. He was sure the men's bathroom didn't come equipped with changing tables, and though it seemed somewhat unsanitary, Vera suggested he go ahead and use the front counter to accomplish the task, and offered to do it for him, for which he was extremely grateful. He paid close attention to which direction she pulled the tapes and actually preened some more when all the women in the store flocked to coo over the baby and him.

Normally this would have honed right in on his natural flirting abilities, perhaps even behooved him to make a date with one of the great-looking gals in the store.

The problem was, the attention he was getting didn't seem to appeal. The only woman he wanted attention from was Dora. And she was off-limits.

And that was too bad. Had she been anybody else, he would have enjoyed the relationship they could have had while she was here, a no-strings, adult association between a man and a woman who knew the score and just wanted to spend a little intimate time while circumstances threw them together under the same roof.

But Dora didn't know the score. For all her grit and spirit, she was still an innocent. And Ethan steered clear of innocents.

He paid for his purchases and retrieved Katie, who was dry and happy. "So where is Vern?" he asked.

"Over at Brewers with the rest of the guys."

"With the—" Oh, no. Dora was over there, too. An innocent chick just ripe for those four old silver foxes to pounce on and plant ideas. They wanted women and babies in town, and once they realized he wasn't going to be the easy prey they'd hoped for, they'd likely try to match Dora up with some other worthy cowboy.

He told himself his hurry was strictly for Dora. He owed it to her to save her from the well-intended meddlers. They could be as tenacious as a determined bull after a rodeo clown.

"Thanks for the diaper change, Vera. I'll catch you later."

Once he'd stowed his purchases in the Cadillac, he

admonished Katie to leave his hat be and entered Brewer's Saloon. There were quite a few customers in for lunch. He waved at Maedean who was expertly carrying burger-laden trays through the maze of tables covered in red-and-white-checked cloths. He looked around the room but didn't see Dora.

From behind the chest-high bar, Iris Brewer hailed him. "Ethan!"

He made his way over to her, still searching the booths and tables. "Hey, Iris. Business is booming."

"That it is. I tell you, I had my reservations about what Lloyd and Ozzie and the boys did with all their advertising, but I've got to say the resurrection of this town is quite exciting. And my cash register is happy." She reached right across the bar, cupped Katie's pudgy cheeks in her hands and gave a gentle kiss. "I was hoping to see this little lamb again."

"Again?"

"Yes. The night of the auction. I minded her while Dora came in and bid on you."

Did the whole town know *everything* about his business? He'd known there would be speculation, but evidently it hadn't fully hit him just how uncomfortable it would make him to have folks privy to details before he even had them. "I see."

"You're looking for Dora, I'd imagine."

"Yes."

"She's in the back with the men."

Playing pool, probably. A set of swinging saloon doors separated the dining room and bar from the game room. A jukebox was in the front, but speakers and dance floors flowed into both rooms so folks could two-step between food courses or pool sets. "Thanks, Iris."

"Uh, Ethan. Why don't you let me take Katie for you?"

He grinned, realizing Iris was dying to get her hands on the baby, and handed Katie over. Iris had lost her daughter and grandson, Timmy Malone—several years back, and everyone knew how her arms had ached to hold a child again. Thankfully, Hannah Richmond had come to town with her four-year-old son, Ian, and was six months pregnant, to boot. She'd married Wyatt Malone and appointed Iris honorary grandmother. Hannah and Wyatt's family had been some of the best medicine for the town.

And of course the four old fellas had taken full credit for the union.

Ethan pushed through the swinging saloon doors but didn't spot Dora at the pool table. The arrangement of the room was different, and it took him a moment to realize just what he was seeing.

The far corner had been cordoned off with a crimson rope and a sign proclaiming it the cigar section.

And there was Dora, smack-dab in the middle of the action, smoking a fat cigar with the four matchmakers of Shotgun Ridge...*and* the preacher!

His brows shot up so fast his hat shifted, and he felt a swift jolt of jealousy as she leaned in and laughed at something Pastor Dan Lucas said. Dan was young, decent looking and single. A preacher and a preacher's daughter was a much better match than a playboy cowboy and a preacher's daughter.

He frowned, wondering if Ozzie and his cronies were thinking the very same thing.

Ethan had to wonder if his playboy persona had somehow undergone a polar metamorphosis due to the broadsides he'd experienced lately. Because he was having an awful lot of prudish, judgmental thoughts where Dora Watkins was concerned.

First finding it inappropriate for her to watch a perfectly natural part of nature—horses mating. And now…well, now he just wasn't sure what to think.

Smoking with the preacher, of all things.

The woman was just full of surprises. And did she have to lean in quite that close to the holy man?

He stepped up behind her.

"You don't like the taste of beer, but you'll smoke a cigar?" he asked, the astonishment underlined with an unfortunate hint of censure.

She whirled around. "Ethan!" She hopped up to grab another chair, her beaming smile completely without guile. "Where's Katie?"

"With Iris. Evidently she didn't think a baby's lungs should be exposed to cigar smoke."

"And well they shouldn't," Ozzie said. "You bet. It's why Lloyd here set up a special section. You bet."

Ethan sat down, shook hands with the preacher—grudgingly—and eyed the old men warily. He didn't trust all four of them in one place. They'd likely talk him into another crazy auction or something.

"Ingenious idea, don't you think, Ethan?" Lloyd asked, indicating the smoking tables with a sweep of his meaty hand. "I tell you, with all the women showing up, the cowboys are flocking here by the droves. Been the best thing for business. We thought up this smoking-room thing, and danged if the women aren't partakin', too!''

Ethan looked at Dora. "So I see." He glanced at Dan Lucas, shook his head and succumbed to a grin. "Your congregation know about your secret vices?"

Dan laughed. "Since half of them are here, I imagine they do."

Dora whacked Ethan on the thigh, startling him, and spoke to Dan. "Oh, don't pay any attention to him. He's got rigid and ridiculous ideas of how preachers and preacher's daughters are supposed to conduct themselves. I'm happy to say I've popped a good many of his preconceived bubbles. So, feel free to aid and abet at being human, Dan. We'll reform Ethan yet."

"That sass is going to get you in trouble one of these days," Ethan said to Dora and plucked the cigar out of her hand to take a drag. He nearly choked at the sickeningly sweet taste.

She giggled. "Designer cigars. Lloyd ordered them all the way from a specialty shop in Texas. That one's cherry."

"I figured that out." When his gaze locked onto hers, he couldn't seem to look away. She wasn't like any woman he'd ever met, and that made him nervous. "Seems I recall someone offering to spring for ice cream. Suppose we ought to go retrieve Katie and get some lunch?"

"Sounds good to me." She stood. "Gentlemen,

thank you for the fine company and hospitality. We'll do it again soon?''

"You bet," Ozzie said.

"Church on Sunday," Dan reminded.

"We'll be there."

As they walked away, Ozzie poked Vern in the ribs and gave a discreet kick beneath the table to Lloyd and Henry. All four men shared a smug look while Dora and Ethan pushed through the swinging doors.

"Fine-lookin' couple," Ozzie commented. "We done it up right."

"Well, I'm all for taking credit," Henry said. "But you have to admit that fate had as much to do with this as we did, with her daddy calling to check out Ethan just at the right time and all."

"Fate, hell—pardon me, Dan," Ozzie said. "Was the Lord's work, is what it was." And his sweet Vanessa's, but Ozzie figured he'd just keep that part private. "That little filly comes from fine stock, you bet. I know her gramps, Quentin. Served with him in the war, I did. And you can call it coincidence with Dora's daddy callin' and all, but if you'll remember correctly, it was us who took care of the timing and got her to the auction."

"Good thing she had some bidding experience and enough spunk and money to follow through," Lloyd said with a barely suppressed shudder. "I suffered a real bad patch there for a few minutes."

"Now, Lloyd." Vern blew out a stream of cigar smoke. "Don't go getting your blood pressure all out of whack again. We already told you that boy was biddin' on Ethan to go on a date with his sister."

Henry and Lloyd snorted, Dan smiled and Ozzie held up a hand to bring the conversation back to the main focus.

"Did you see how those youngsters were eatin' each other up with their eyes?"

"Ethan and Dora?" Henry asked, just to be sure they were all on the same subject.

"Of course Ethan and Dora." He glared around the table, wondering if he was the only one paying attention. Vanessa, God rest her soul, used to tell him he had the most astonishing blue eyes, and that their very uniqueness could command an audience. Evidently he wasn't using his God-given qualities to their fullest.

"The boy don't seem to know he's a goner...yet. But he'll figure it out soon enough. Yep, Dora Watkins is just the thing for Ethan Callahan. You bet."

"Now, Ozzie." Dan figured he ought to inject the voice of reason. "Matchmaking is commendable on occasion, but you have to be realistic and realize that there are other factors at work. A child's future is involved."

"Well of course it is!" Ozzie burst out, drawing the attention of a couple of women at the pool table. He lowered his voice. "I'm surprised at you, the very preacher, being such a killjoy. Where's your faith? I tell you, if you ain't performing a ceremony of marriage in a few weeks' time, I'll...well, I'll eat this here cigar. And the boys'll swallow theirs, too." If there was one thing Ozzie Peyton was good at, it was dragging his buddies right along with him—for their own good, of course.

Chapter Nine

Dora looked out the kitchen window, riveted by the sight of Ethan, shirtless, his Stetson-covered head tipped back as he poured a cooling canteen of water over his bare, rippling chest. Her breath suspended in her throat and her heart clamored. There ought to be a law against a man possessing that much provocative, spine-tingling sexuality.

Absently she turned on the kitchen tap and ran cool water over her wrists.

Katie was napping, and since she had work to do in the dark room, Dora had offered to stay inside and listen for the baby so Ethan could go out and deal with some of the ranch duties. But *she* wasn't getting much work done staring at him this way.

She wanted him to understand the responsibilities of a single parent, but she also wanted him to see the merits of sharing those responsibilities. With a loved one—not a baby-sitter.

And to that end she decided it was time to make sure he didn't in any way view her as a baby-sitter.

And getting the attention of a man like Ethan Callahan would require clever seduction. So, how hard could that be?

The wall phone in the kitchen rang and she automatically answered. "Callahan & Sons ranch."

"It's a dark day indeed when a minister lets his daughter go off into a den of iniquity."

"Grandpa!" Delighted, Dora twined the phone cord around her fingers and settled back against the counter, glad to have something else to focus on besides Ethan's blissfully glistening chest muscles. "How are you?"

"Concerned is how I am. Why is it when I call to check on my favorite granddaughter, I have to find out secondhand that she's living with three men?"

"I'm your only granddaughter," she pointed out.

"And have standards to uphold because of it," he groused, love shining through the bluster in his voice. "Playboys, the lot of them, I hear. How's that sweet little Katie?"

"Growing," Dora said, a sudden cloud passing over the sunshine of her spirits.

With a shrewdness that made Quentin Watkins the powerful man he was, he picked right up on her undertones. "What's going on, peaches?"

Tears caught in her throat when he called her that nickname in his soft, gruff tone. How many times had he used that loving voice on her? *Come tell Grandpa what's wrong, peaches, and I'll fix it.*

But Grandpa couldn't fix the uncertainty of Dora and Katie's future.

"Nothing's going on, Grandpa."

"Now, I'm gonna have to speak with that daddy

of yours. Devout man of God not impressing upon his children the merits of honesty. Drummed that virtue into you myself, I did.''

Dora smiled. ''It's good to hear your voice, Grandpa. I've missed you.''

''Well.'' He cleared his throat. ''Heard from a buddy of mine right there in Shotgun Ridge. You've met up with Ozzie Peyton, have you?''

''Yes. He's wonderful.''

''Flew B-17s with me back in forty-two. Quite a belly gunner.''

''Mmm.'' Ozzie had told her the same, although he'd expounded more on Grandpa's piloting skill.

''So, this Ethan Callahan…he the one who's put that heaviness in your voice?''

''It's not—''

''Peaches, it's me you're talkin' to here.''

Dora sighed. ''Ethan's a good man, Grandpa. And he's Katie's father.'' She ignored his censorious harrumph. She imagined Quentin Watkins had already gotten the full story from her father. ''I'm in love with him.''

The declaration brought with it several seconds of dead air on the telephone lines. ''Mighty quick, don't you think?''

''You fell in love with Grandma at first sight,'' she countered.

''And married her a week later, don't forget. Didn't go having her move in with me till there was a certificate of marriage all right and proper. So just what are Ethan Callahan's intentions, I want to know.''

Dora couldn't help but smile, even though Ethan's

intentions were somewhat of a pesky mystery. The only thing for certain was that the "preacher's daughter" label he'd assigned to her scared him silly.

"I'm not living with him, Grandpa. He's getting to know his daughter."

Quentin harrumphed again in skepticism. "I've a mind to fly out there and see for myself. Those boys got a landing strip on that fancy breedin' ranch?"

"A small one. You can't fly in here, Grandpa."

He misunderstood. "What kind of an operation is it, I'd like to know, if you can't even land a Lear?"

"You can land a Lear, Grandpa. But you won't."

"I won't?"

"No. I'm fine and I have a plan."

"Now there's the granddaughter I raised so well. Why didn't you say so in the first place."

Dora laughed. "I just did. Now say goodbye, Grandpa."

"You call me, hear?"

"I'll call you." She replaced the phone with a smile. Good thing he didn't press her on her plans. She didn't think an admission that seduction was her strategy would go over well with Quentin Watkins. He'd be in the Lear within the half hour.

DORA'S ATTEMPTS at seduction were failing miserably. She was beginning to think she needed to take a page out of the horse-breeding manual and attempt a teasing-rail experiment of her own, because Ethan definitely wasn't responding to anything else. Every time she got close enough to touch, he practically ran in the opposite direction.

And she had no earthly idea what she was doing wrong.

She'd yet to get him sufficiently worked up enough to have him participating in another of those kisses she'd managed to initiate last week.

The way he was acting, you'd think she was wearing a nun's habit or something.

Bewildered, she leaned against the stark white wood railing by the exercise corral. Clay had Katie perched on his shoulder as he supervised the cooling down of a recently ridden mare. Grant stood close by, supervising Clay's handling of Katie. That made her smile.

The activity of the ranch wasn't as busy today for some reason. She wondered where Ethan was. Each day he got more proficient at balancing his ranching with Katie and was no longer chained to the house. And Katie had charmed every man on the ranch. Between her uncles and the ranch hands, there were plenty of willing arms to hold her, thus freeing up Ethan's time.

Time and privacy he could have put to good use if he would just notice that Dora was available and willing.

She ran her hands over her butt, checking to see if her panty lines showed beneath the tight material of her jeans. A masculine groan sounded right behind her, and she whipped around in time to see Ethan staring…and frowning.

Ah, progress. Delighted, she gave a small test and rubbed again.

His frown deepened. ''Did you hurt yourself?''

She nearly stamped her foot. And she certainly wasn't the type of woman to enact such a display. Four brothers had bedeviled that trait right out of her. But darn it all, she wasn't used to being such a dismal failure at anything she attempted.

"No," she answered at last. "Just adjusting."

He looked away, actually took a step farther to the left instead of moving next to her.

Dora sighed and gave up for now. "Any luck with Warrior and Sunday Best?"

"Not yet. She's in heat, but she's not interested in the stud."

"Maybe one of them's just playing hard to get," she suggested. Ethan ought to understand that perfectly. And in this case, rather than siding with Sunday Best, Dora fully commiserated with Warrior.

"Hard to tell. But I don't like to force something like this. Those animals are too valuable to risk injury to either one of them, or to the handlers."

"So what'll you do?"

"Nothing for today. In fact, we're due over at a neighbor's ranch to help him out with his branding."

"Cattle?"

"Yeah. This time of year all the neighbors rotate and trade services, working each other's ranches. My brothers and I'll take our men over to Wyatt Malone's and give him a hand, and he'll bring his wrestlers over here once we get our herd rounded up."

"Here? You're going to herd cows over here and mix them with your horses?" She looked around at the white wood fences and green, green grass. Everything seemed so...*orderly*. The image of cattle crowded in pens, dust flying, wouldn't quite gel in Dora's mind.

"No, we won't bring them in this close. We've got most of them parked on another section of land about five miles south of here. We'll castrate and brand out there."

"Cast—" She shook her head, decided not to finish that query. "I hadn't realized you had such a big operation. When do you find time to play?"

And when do you find time to respond to a woman and fall in love?

"Different times of the year are less busy. And since Grant and Clay and I are equal partners here, we've got more freedom than the next guy."

She gave him what she hoped was a look of invitation. He didn't seem to notice.

"Uh, back to the branding, though. It's something I'd committed to before Katie...and you."

So this is why he'd sought her out, when he'd been doing his level best to avoid her for the past few days.

"What?" she said with a hint of challenge in her voice. "Need a baby-sitter?" This was just the kind of thing she'd counted on—the kind of thing to get him to realize raising a child alone wasn't an easy feat.

He sighed. "Yes. I could ask Hannah—Wyatt's wife—to watch her." He shrugged, casually leaned an elbow atop the fence. "Or you could come with me. Meet the neighbors."

Her heart gave a somersault, and an odd feeling came over her. He was looking at her strangely... hopefully even. Although she could be wrong about that. She wasn't exactly at the head of her class in her attempts to read his signals.

But somehow, asking her to meet the neighbors sounded a whole lot like asking her to meet his parents.

And although he didn't have parents and it probably was only her imagination getting carried away with her and was nothing of the kind, she wanted to meet Wyatt and Hannah Malone. Especially Hannah.

She had some questions that only another woman could answer.

"Sure. Katie and I would love to come."

IN ETHAN'S TRUCK, with Katie strapped in her car seat in the back seat of the extended cab, Dora drank in the beauty of the endless prairie, where grass and wildflowers waved in the breeze and cattle grazed on the abundant landscape.

"If you're going to brand and do unspeakable things to Wyatt's cows, how come they're still spread out like this?" They were traveling in a caravan with white, Callahan & Sons pickups in front and behind them.

"Those are my cattle. We're still on Callahan land, will be for another ten miles or so."

"Did your dad already own all this, or did you add to it after the inheritance?"

"We've picked up another ten thousand acres since then."

She had so many questions she didn't know in which order to ask them. Everything about Ethan's life and the town and neighbors he loved intrigued her.

"So what kind of guy is Wyatt Malone that he has to advertise for a mail-order bride?"

Ethan grinned. "He didn't advertise. The old matchmakers did that all on their own. Wyatt was shocked as all get-out when he went into town for his regular Thursday-night dinner and ended up taking home a pregnant woman and her kid."

"That must have been uncomfortable for Hannah."

"She didn't know. She thought Wyatt had sent for her. She answered the ad and Ozzie wrote back, pretending to be Wyatt."

"He ought to be ashamed."

Ethan laughed. "If there's one thing those fellas have very little of, it's shame. Anyway, Hannah's husband was a creep and a womanizer. When he got her pregnant the second time, he opted out and took off with some bimbo to Jamaica."

"*Creep* is too mild a word."

"Mmm. My sentiments exactly. Anyway, Wyatt was totally blown away when Hannah presented him with a copy of the magazine advertisement he'd supposedly placed, inviting her to come out and marry him. He's got a big heart and couldn't just turn her away, so he took her home. Besides, he took one look at four-year-old Ian and fell instantly in love with the little guy."

"With her boy and not her?"

"Oh, I think he fell for her just as quick and hard, but it took him a while longer to figure that out." He went silent for a minute. "Wyatt had a soft spot in his heart for Ian, though, because the boy reminded him of what his own son would have looked like had he lived.''

"Oh, he lost a child?"

Ethan nodded. "And his wife. Died in a car accident not far from the ranch. He wasn't interested in replacing that family, but Hannah and Ian were hard to resist."

"I imagine it was a bit awkward once Hannah found out Wyatt hadn't actually sent for her."

"Total understatement. She wanted to leave right away, but she'd packed up her entire life in the back of a rented trailer and come out here thinking she'd be starting over in a new life." He gave a soft chuckle. "Then Wyatt had a bright idea of trying to fix her up with another cowboy in the area so she could have her dream."

"But Wyatt was her dream," Dora guessed.

"And she, his, as it turns out."

"You know an awful lot about it—and him."

"Wyatt and I have been friends and neighbors since we were boys—since I came here. I was his son's godfather."

She reached across the cab of the truck and laid her hand on his arm. "Oh, Ethan. I'm sorry."

"Thanks. It was tough. Timmy was about Katie's age when the accident happened."

She saw him glance in the mirror at the baby in the car seat, felt the muscles of his arms go rigid for an instant. He was probably imagining the same fate befalling Katie, reliving the choking incident again. She gave his arm a comforting squeeze.

"So were you on Wyatt's list of eligible cowboys for Hannah?"

This question clearly lightened his mood. "No way. He was pea-green jealous every time I looked at her."

Dora frowned. "Did you *want* to be on the list?"

"Me?" He chuckled. "Consider matrimony? No way."

His careless comment stung her heart, even though she knew he hadn't intended it to. Ethan Callahan didn't believe in marriage. He'd already told her as much.

Her battle was definitely going to be an uphill one.

"I'll have to admit, though," he continued. "I did abet in the scheme against my buddy. Never thought I'd do such a thing—especially to a friend—but any fool could see he was crazy about Hannah and Ian. And he was as protective of that baby in her womb as if it was his own."

Dora sighed. "What a wonderful man."

He glanced at her. "What about me? Don't you think it was pretty wonderful of me to help out, too?"

That ego was going to get him in trouble one of these days. And it was one of the things she loved about him. But she certainly couldn't let on that she felt that way.

"You're just a regular saint," she said dryly, then realized that was a very poor choice of words when his brows snapped together.

She sighed and told herself not to notice the strength of his hands wrapped around the steering wheel, not to wonder what they would feel like holding her close. And she absolutely would not speculate on his thighs or his belt buckle, or the terribly inappropriate image that popped in her head of him wearing only a cowboy hat. Nothing else.

She shifted in her seat, adjusted the air-conditioning vent and focused on their surroundings. Off to the right there were two long lines of cattle moving down a knoll and across the prairie grass like ants heading for the holiday pies. A half dozen horsemen were scattered around the herd. She wondered if the young bulls would have been behaving so nicely if they knew what was in store for them.

"This is it," Ethan said as they turned off the main road and passed under the arched Double M sign.

"Oh, my. You cowboys *are* partial to large spreads."

"You're impressed?" he asked, a hint of petulance in his tone—obviously because it was his *neighbor's* spread she was commenting on and not his.

Dora hid a smile. "Absolutely." The ranch house was a huge, two-story structure. Where Ethan's property was all flowing lines of pristine white against a backdrop of verdant green, the Double M was predominantly red. Trees had been planted for shade and a windbreak. Not far from the main outbuildings, cows pushed together in corrals, bawling and kicking up plenty of dust.

"That's Wyatt."

Mercy, Dora thought. Cowboys sure were bred right, out here in Shotgun Ridge. Wyatt Malone was as gorgeous as the Callahan brothers. He had his arm around his very pregnant wife and held a little boy perched on his shoulder.

Ethan parked the truck, and Dora got Katie out of the back.

"Uncle Ethan!" The little boy, wearing miniature boots and a cowboy hat wiggled down from Wyatt and ran to Ethan.

"Ian," Hannah admonished. "At least let him get out of the truck."

Ethan caught the boy on the fly and lifted him into his arms. "Hey there, sport. You been behaving?"

"Yep. My dad gived me my very own horse, and I have to take good care of her."

Dora noticed that Ethan listened attentively to the child, yet his gaze met Wyatt's when the boy called Wyatt his dad. There was something very special going on here, and the Malones, as well as Ethan, all responded with soft looks that clearly spoke of a closeness born of the heart rather than blood.

"Your dad's a smart man," Ethan said, setting Ian back on the ground. "He knows every cowboy should own a horse by the time he's four."

"Yep. And I'm four."

Ethan ruffled Ian's hair and stepped toward Hannah. "Hey there, California. Wanna ditch this cattleman and run off with me?"

Wyatt rolled his eyes, and Hannah laughed as she easily moved into Ethan's arms and kissed him. Dora felt a jolt of envy as he put his hand over Hannah's pregnant tummy.

At that moment he looked up, and his gaze locked

with Dora's. It was a look rife with unspoken emotions, which Dora had no experience reading.

"Hannah and Wyatt, this is Dora Watkins...and my daughter, Katie."

The Malones didn't even blink. Chances were the grapevine had already reached them, and they knew all about the auction and the baby.

Wyatt confirmed this with a sexy grin that had his wife staring for a split instant. The responsiveness, the deep love evident between the two was touching.

"Heard you paid a pretty steep price for this old cowboy," Wyatt said.

"Watch who you're calling old," Ethan complained, and moved to Dora's side, rescuing his hat when Katie tried to snatch it off.

Dora laughed. "Actually, I was only acting as agent for Katie, here."

Hannah stepped forward. "You men go on and take care of those poor cattle so they don't have to wait around in anticipation any longer than necessary." She gave a delicate shudder, obviously knowing what the men intended. "Dora and I will go have coffee and talk about the two of you."

"Hey, I think I like the kitchen agenda better than what's out here," Ethan said.

Dora gave him a sassy look. "Too bad. No boys invited."

He hooked a finger under her chin, tipped her face up to his. "Who said anything about boys?" His voice was deep and soft and rich with suggestion.

Dora's heart nearly stopped. Right there in front of the neighbors, he might as well have shouted that he was a man and knew exactly what to do with his masculinity.

The problem was, Dora didn't know what to do with his masculinity.

Which was her prime objective for accompanying him today.

She cleared her throat, stepped back. Now she was the one who felt like running, but it couldn't be helped. They had an audience. And she truly needed a better grasp on the rules and intricacies of her situation.

Still, she couldn't just let him get the last word. Her brothers would be ashamed of her. "You want to talk about sex, cowboy?" she asked softly.

He reacted as typically as she'd expected and jolted as though someone had goosed him with the branding iron.

"One of these days I'm going to call that bluff, legs." He tugged his hat low on his forehead. "Let's don't stand around all day, Malone. We've got cattle to see to."

"Well, that was very interesting," Hannah said when the men walked away. "May I?" She held out her hands toward Katie.

Dora passed the baby girl to Hannah. "I apologize for that bold conversation. We've just met, and you probably think I'm a hussy or something." Actually, Dora was horrified that she'd let her quick tongue get away from her in front of virtual strangers.

"No. I think you're probably just perfect."

The look that passed between them told Dora that Hannah was someone she could trust, and she immediately, happily dropped her guard again. "Ethan's apparently allergic to me."

"I doubt that. Billy! Don't you even think of touching my garden!"

Dora looked around for another child and saw a goat, instead. It trotted right over and nuzzled against Hannah's dress as though seeking forgiveness.

"Ian, honey, would you put Billy back on his leash for momma?"

The little boy happily wrapped his arms around the goat's neck and urged it away from the house. Dora wished she had her camera or her sketch pad. Boy and goat were precious together.

She glanced back at Hannah. "Family pet?" Although Hannah bossed the animal around, she seemed just a bit apprehensive.

"The silly thing adopted me the minute I set foot on this ranch. We've come to somewhat of an understanding since then." She laughed. "You'll have heard that I came here to be Wyatt's mail-order bride."

Dora bit her bottom lip. "Mmm. Unbeknownst to him."

Hannah held open the back door and let Dora precede her into the kitchen. "Poor guy. I practically landed on his doorstep, determined to be a ranch wife...and scared to death of all the animals."

"Looks like you're doing a good job of overcoming your fears."

"Yes. It's a matter of attitude. Sometimes mine wavers."

"And the goat takes advantage."

"Pitiful, isn't it? Have a seat. I'll get the coffee." She waved Dora to the kitchen table and set Katie on the floor, giving the baby a plastic bowl and wooden spoon to play with. "I'm short on toys, but what kid doesn't like to beat on the dishes?"

Dora smiled, admiring Hannah's ease and improvisation. "So, you're from California?" Dora asked.

"Yes."

"Would you mind if I asked you a really strange question?"

"Of course not." She measured fragrant, finely ground beans into the percolator.

"How familiar are you with herbs and alternative health stuff, like which foods are aphrodisiacs."

"Aphrodisiacs?" Hannah sputtered, laughing happily.

Dora nodded.

"For what?"

"I want to feed them to Ethan."

Clearly astonished, she paused and turned fully to face Dora. "To Ethan?"

Dora nodded again.

"Are we talking about the same cowboy here? Six-three or better? Consummate flirt? Too handsome for his own good?"

"One and the same."

"Well, I'll be."

"So, do you have any suggestions?"

"I'm sorry to say I never really studied herbs or their…uh, *effects* on the libido."

"Then in that case, I'm in dire need of tips on how to seduce the man."

Forgetting all about the coffee, Hannah sat. "I see."

"I'm in love with Ethan," she said in a rush, lest Hannah think she was some sort of free-and-easy type woman, after all.

"I came here to fulfill a promise to Katie's mother, and to convince Ethan to give me custody of the baby because she's like a daughter to me. But all that's changed and it's the biggest mess. I certainly didn't plan on falling in love with him, but there it is."

"And this is a problem," Hannah said, her tone suggesting she did indeed understand and commiserate.

"Yes. Ethan's got some crazy hang-up about me being a preacher's daughter and all. So if I wait for him to make the first move, I'll likely be old and gray. The problem is, I seem to be doing something wrong."

"Looked to me like he was responding just fine out there in the yard."

"Oh, sure. For two seconds. That's about how long it takes him to remember who he's flirting with." She flicked her hair behind her ear and reached out to steady Katie as the child levered herself to her feet using Dora's thigh as a pulley.

"To be perfectly honest, Hannah, I don't have any…uh, hands-on experience in this sort of thing. Seduction, and…sex, that is. And for a man like Ethan Callahan, that's what it's going to take to get his attention."

"And you want me to coach you?"

Dora let out a breath. Even woman-to-woman, this conversation was difficult. "If you wouldn't mind."

The smile that spread across Hannah's face was full of unholy feminine glee. "Oh, this is going to be fun." And Hannah Malone couldn't wait to tell her husband that Ethan Callahan, heartbreaker playboy cowboy, was actually resisting a woman!

Chapter Ten

For the past week Ethan felt like a stallion that was constantly being led to the teasing rail, yet never allowed to follow through. He wasn't sleeping, he couldn't concentrate on his work, and he didn't know what to do about it.

His life was in chaos. And it was Dora's fault.

She decorated his life with the simple effervescence of her sunny personality. She bebopped to music through her headphones, or if she wasn't wearing them, just to the beat in her head. She flitted through the day like a butterfly, rarely resting. She'd set something down, forget about it and step right over it without a care.

It wasn't as though she considered herself a princess or expected others to pick up after her. She simply didn't notice, wasn't bothered. She appeared to exist in her own bubble.

Yet she wasn't a woman a man should underestimate. She was sharp.

And obviously determined to seduce him.

Which was why he was lurking in the hall like a

coward, checking the television room to see if she was there, to see if he needed to head in the opposite direction.

His heart jolted when he saw her, but Ethan didn't run. Instead he leaned against the doorjamb and grinned.

Clay had the misfortune of thinking he could take a quick snooze in his favorite easy chair. He lay there unsuspectingly, reared back in the recliner, his legs crossed, blissfully unaware of what was happening around him.

Dora leaned over him, carefully positioning a kitten and a puppy—a border collie pup Ethan didn't recognize—on the back of the chair by Clay's shoulders.

Quickly, professionally, Dora stepped back and started clicking away with the camera.

And that's when all hell broke loose.

The kitten batted at Clay's hair, startling him awake, which in turn startled the animals.

Clay came up out of the chair cursing, the cat shot off the recliner, climbed straight up the wall unit and knocked over Grant's rodeo trophy, and the dog snatched the paperback book Clay had been reading and shimmied under the sofa.

Thoroughly entertained—especially since he wasn't the unsuspecting victim this time—Ethan quickly swooped up Katie before the puppy could mow her down as it tore out from under the sofa again, barking happily at the fun game. Max, wearing the canine equivalent of a mature, put-upon expression, guarded Ethan's leg and the baby.

"What the hell?" Still in a half stupor from sleep, Clay blinked like a barn owl.

"Language," Ethan admonished.

"Beg pardon." The angry expression cleared from Clay's face as he looked at Dora, realized at last what was going on.

"I'm sorry," Dora said, eyes shining with mirth. "I couldn't resist that shot."

She wasn't a bit sorry, Ethan thought, a strange, indulgent warmth invading his senses. He was starting to look forward to her unpredictability.

"Oh…uh, that's okay." Clay looked warily at the kitten perched on the top shelf of the wall unit.

Dora didn't seem concerned.

"I don't believe I recognize these animals," Ethan commented casually, shifting Katie in his arms when she wiggled to get down.

"Aren't they darling? I got them from Hannah."

Ethan's brows rose. "Justine's pups and our own barn cats weren't good enough?"

"Oh, they're wonderful. But each animal has its own individual personality and expression."

"Mmm. And these two are full of spit and vinegar." Good thing Wyatt had gotten rid of the llama, or she'd have probably dragged that home, too.

"Makes a nice variety." She glanced up to the top shelf of the wall unit. "Suppose we should get her down, or let her find her own way?"

"Is she house broken?"

"Right. We'll get her."

Clay was one step ahead of them. He'd already scooped up the squirming puppy and was coaxing the wiry kitty with a wiggle of his fingers, which worked like a charm. He laughed when the puppy started licking him to death. "I'll take them out with the other baby animals if that's okay?"

Ethan looked at Dora, wondering if she would put up a fuss, but she nodded in agreement. Probably because she knew they kept the pups and kittens in the stable next to the tack room, all nice and cozy with all the comforts an animal could want. Manny took excellent care of them.

"So, are these *new* pets we've acquired, or are we hopefully just borrowing them?"

"Just borrowing. I feel as though I'm in Heaven out here. Usually I have to go to the pound to get animals, then there's the problem of finding them a good home." She picked up a throw pillow that had been knocked on the floor and tossed it back on the couch. Ethan blinked.

"The people at church have been good about adopting," she continued, obviously unaware that she'd actually noticed something out of place, "so it really works out very well all the way around—for the most part. There are a couple of the older animals who've become wards of the church."

Ethan felt a smile tug. "A couple?"

"Well, maybe more like a few."

Her tinkling laugh charmed him. And though he knew he ought to just cut this conversation off, he couldn't seem to walk away. She was driving him nuts, but he wanted to be with her. Problem was, he wanted to be with her really badly, as close as a man and woman could get. And that was a dangerous way to be thinking in a house full of beds.

"Do you ride?"

"Horses? Of course."

"What do you say we go out tomorrow, let you see a little of the place, maybe have lunch down by the creek? We'll rig Katie up in the backpack and you can bring your sketch pad," he said quickly so it wouldn't sound like he was asking her for a date. "You can draw the butterflies or something."

She looked at him for a very long moment, and Ethan wanted to take back the invitation. There was a fire in her lake-blue eyes, and something more. An attitude, he realized, one that any man past puberty would recognize and respond to. It was in the way she dipped her head and cocked it slightly to the left, the way she touched her throat, slowly shifted her hair, the way she looked directly into his eyes and held him there.

She dragged her teeth across her bottom lip leaving a sheen that made him swallow hard.

"A picnic?" Her whisky voice was soft, like a sensuously whispered melody, but it still jolted him, made him aware of where he was and that he had a baby in his arms and a firm vow to keep his hands to himself.

His brows drew together. "Are you doing that deliberately?"

"Yes." Just like that. No coyness. No pretending to misunderstand. She breezed past him on her way to the door, then doubled back and gave Katie a gentle kiss.

When her eyes raised to his, Ethan found that he'd gone mute, paralyzed and mesmerized all over again.

"And I'd love to go on a picnic with you, Ethan." Her lips brushed the corner of his mouth. "I'll see you in the morning."

It was a full five seconds before Ethan remembered to breathe. He rested his jaw on top of Katie's head, feeling a tug at his heart when he glanced down and saw her pudgy cheek pressed against his chest, her normally energized eyes heavy with sleepiness.

"I think I just made a big mistake, kiddo."

DORA DRESSED CAREFULLY in figure-hugging jeans and a white tank top that barely reached her waist-band. If she moved ever so subtly, the hemline of the top exposed flirty glimpses of bare skin.

"Okay, Katie, how do I look?" She lifted the baby's foot and pretended to gnaw on her toes, which sent Katie into gales of heartwarming giggles, her mouth wide open, her cheeks so round they looked as if they would meet her eyebrows.

Scooping her up, Dora did a little dance around the room, allowing herself the pure pleasure of just holding the little girl, smelling her baby-powder-scented skin, pressing her lips to that sweet spot just there on the child's neck.

"I don't think I could stand it if I lost you, Katie," she murmured. "I love you so much." Realizing she was about to get weepy, Dora took a breath and added a note of excitement to her voice. "Yep, I do. Now, we're going for a horseback ride. What do you say about that? And you, my little munchkin, get to ride with me in your backpack. Kind of like putting a saddle on me, huh?''

She finished packing the diaper bag and skipped down the stairs, her laughter blending with Katie's as the child shrieked and clapped over the bouncy ride. ''You like that? You'll do just fine on the horse, then.''

Stopping on her way through the kitchen, Dora grabbed her camera and sketch pad and stuffed both in the diaper bag, then loaded the small picnic basket. ''Just let him try and resist my fried chicken,'' she said as they went out the kitchen door.

It was a glorious day for a picnic.

And for seduction.

Oh, she knew this wouldn't be *the* time. But at least she could try to lay the groundwork. Overcome his objections.

Perhaps even make him fall in love.

She sighed and stepped into the cool interior of the stables.

The smell of horses, hay, leather and liniment mingled together and swirled on the breeze. For some reason the scent reminded her of money. Crazy, she thought. Grandpa had done a fine job of teaching Dora the value of property and to recognize the signs of success, which was likely where the equation came from.

And in here there were plenty of signs of success. The sloped concrete floor was swept clean, the stalls lined with fresh straw or sawdust. Blankets, buckets and all manner of implements were tidily grouped and organized. And they all bore the Callahan & Sons green-and-white logo, right down to the last curry brush.

Ethan was checking the cinch on the saddle of a pretty roan mare. She paused, trying not to make a sound, wanting to take a moment just to admire him—not just his devastatingly handsome looks, but the way he lovingly ran his hand over the roan's sleek neck, the capability that emanated from him. The muscles in his arms and shoulders bunched as he went about his work, spoke with Manny and Grant, lifted a stallion's leg and conferred with another man Dora didn't recognize over the horse's shoe.

Katie, having been uncannily, blessedly quiet up to that point, squealed, kicking her legs and waving her arms as Max trotted over to them. "Ax!"

Ethan looked up, and right away told himself to get a grip. With her blond hair haloed by a backdrop of sunlight, she looked like an angel. And for a stunning second he could have sworn he saw her glow.

It was an image he needed to remember, to remind himself of, about every two seconds for the next little while, or more likely the rest of his life.

Thou shalt not touch the preacher's daughter, he chanted silently.

The admonishment didn't do a bit of good when she was the one doing the touching. She walked right up to him and placed her hand on his arm, gave it a firm squeeze.

"I'm going to admit something, so brace yourself."

He did, surprised by the way his heart bumped

against his chest. There was no telling what this maddening, unpredictable woman was going to say.

"I'm impressed."

He was a goner. That's all there was to it.

A grin started deep in his gut and flowed all the way to his lips. "I'm crazy about you, legs."

"Well?" The single word was an invitation, as was the lift of her brows and the sassy quirk of her mouth. "Feel free to *show* me how crazy."

Ethan laughed. "Don't even go there."

"Chicken."

"You got that right. Yellow clear through." He kissed Katie's waving hand. Luckily Dora's short height made it too far of a reach for the baby to grab his hat. "Come on. Let's see if I can impress you some more."

He led her to a stall where a darling little foal was enjoying a frisky romp in the spacious area.

"Oh, isn't she a sweetheart."

"She's Katie's."

Dora looked at him, and for a fleeting instant an emotion flared in her eyes that reminded him of sadness. Or fear.

"Don't you think Katie's a little young to have a horse?"

"I'm not going to turn her loose right now." He gave a gentle, playful tug to Dora's hair, glad that the odd expression had passed. "They'll grow up together. By the time Katie's ready, Stony Stratton will have this filly trained to perfection."

"Why Stony and not one of your men? Or you?"

"Because Stony's the best. Remember that Redford movie?"

She nodded.

"Not only could Stony have played the part, he lives it. He's got an uncanny way with animals. It's a gift."

"A horse whisperer?"

"Something like that. Ready?" He led her back to where the horses were saddled. "Meet Clarabelle." He patted the roan on her neck.

"Clarabelle?" Dora repeated.

"Don't let the name fool you. She's got plenty of spirit. But she'll be happy to walk, which is what I figured we'd do today since we have Katie." He placed a step stool beside the horse and steadied Dora and Katie as Dora slipped her foot in the stirrup and mounted. He slid his gaze over the snug fit of her jeans and told himself he was *not* going to notice that flirty patch of smooth skin where her tank top didn't quite meet her waistband.

He checked the length of the stirrups, adjusted them and looked up—right into her blue-eyed gaze. She had some kind of glossy stuff on her voluptuous lips that was going to drive him crazy, make him want to taste.

He cleared his throat. "Okay?"

"Perfect. This feels so good."

He wasn't going to groan. He *wasn't*. And he wasn't going to respond to Grant's or Clay's knowing smiles since they'd very obviously heard Dora's innocent words and placed the same sinful connotation on them that Ethan had.

He tugged his hat low on his brow and mounted his horse. "Clara will respond to the slight pressure of your knees, or a featherlight touch of the reins. She reads minds."

Dora's laugh bubbled up like a clear brook. "She does not."

Ethan shrugged. "See for yourself."

All the way out of the corral and onto the grounds, he kept the pace to a walk, checking Katie often, noticing that the sway of the horse was lulling her. A comfortable silence settled around them as they drank in the smell of fresh-mowed grass, and the sight of white fences that comprised individual pens where purebred mares and their foals grazed. Beyond them stretched miles of prairie and endless blue sky.

Sometimes it still surprised him that all this was his. Who would have thought that a dirty kid who picked pockets on the streets of Chicago would turn out like this, have so much, be so fulfilled. Odd how that last thought nudged him, as though something was missing but he couldn't quite put his finger on it.

He glanced at Katie and Dora, charmed by the look of pure appreciation on Dora's face.

"If I was to say—" Dora's words broke off as Clarabelle halted, her bridle jingling as she tossed her head in a nod. "Stop," Dora finished. "My gosh, she did read my mind! I thought the word stop, and she did."

"Told ya."

"Mmm." She started Clarabelle walking again by staring at a spot between the horse's ears.

Ethan felt a smile bathe his insides with a fire that settled into warmth as it reached his mouth and eyes. Dora had such an enjoyment of life. She was still staring intently at Clarabelle's ears, looking thoroughly pleased with herself, as though she were guiding the horse by telepathy.

Actually it was the unconscious shift of her body a millisecond before her brain caught up and signaled action that Clarabelle was responding to.

"Almost there," he said.

Dora looked up and drew in a breath. "Oh, I had no idea this was here."

Just ahead of them a creek bubbled soothingly over smooth rocks. Typical of June, the cottonwoods were already letting their snow fly, dotting the creek bank with whispy tufts of white.

"I thought you'd like it. Sit tight and I'll help you down with Katie."

Dora was already swinging her leg over the saddle. He might have known she wouldn't wait. It was a wonder she managed to sit still for so long in the first place. A whirlwind rarely rested.

Ethan took Katie out of the backpack, amazed that the kid didn't wake up with all the jostling. After Dora had spread the blanket, he laid the baby down in the shade, smiling at the way she sprawled like a limp frog.

His fingertips lingered over her fine wisps of hair. It continually awed him that this little girl had come from him.

And it frightened him, too.

One of the reasons he appreciated pure bloodlines

was because his were so inferior. What if there was something in his genetic background that could be passed along to an unsuspecting child? It happened in horses. No matter how hard you tried to breed it out of them, certain nasty traits, ones that could be a couple of generations removed would show up.

Had he passed something along to Katie?

What's done was done, he thought, and all he could do now was compensate for any renegade genes. Proper raising could counteract flaws, he reminded himself.

Stony Stratton proved it time and again with his horses.

Fred Callahan had proved it with Ethan and his brothers. Ethan felt he'd turned out to be a pretty good guy despite his faults. He wasn't a drunk or misfit or murderer. His biggest fault was his inability to commit.

Actually, it wasn't an inability. It was a choice.

He was perfectly happy with his life.

"You're deep in thought," Dora said softly from beside him. Her shoulder brushed his as they both gazed down at the sleeping baby on the blanket. "What are you thinking?"

"About flaws and bloodlines and the fact that the responsibility of raising a kid scares me spitless."

"You just work with what you've got, Ethan. One day at a time and with plenty of love."

She was facing him now, had her hand against his chest, over his heart. He imagined her intention at that moment was to soothe.

He didn't feel the least bit calm. And he saw the

minute she realized it, saw the surprise, the satisfaction and the invitation.

He stepped back. "No you don't, legs."

A faint shadow of hurt sparked in her blue eyes, and he realized his evasions appeared like rejections. But before he could backtrack and try to fix the damage—even though he didn't know what the damage was—she smiled, confusing him anew.

"Ethan Callahan, you're disappointing me something fierce, I'll have you know. I hear all this talk about your reputation and come to find it's all lies."

His ego just couldn't let that go. "Well, maybe not *all* of it. Is that fried chicken I smell?"

She opened the basket he'd unstrapped from the back of his saddle. "Mmm-hmm. Does it tempt you?"

He frowned. "Is that a trick question?"

"Excuse me?"

"You know. Like Eve tempting Adam with the apple. Are there strings attached to that chicken?"

"You mean am I attempting to lead you into sin?" She laid out chicken and crusty French bread, olives, a pasta salad and moist brownies. Then she looked up and held his gaze with a provocative intensity that nearly scorched. "Shame on you for thinking such a thing."

Ethan took a deep breath. Her words denied, but her eyes told all. It was going to be a very long lunch.

He sat down on the blanket, bit into the chicken, nearly moaned. "You cooked all this, legs?"

"Surprise you?" She poured lemonade into plastic cups.

"I'm beyond being surprised by you. I think," he amended, and popped an olive in his mouth. Her ability to keep him off balance was an intoxicating, intriguing gift, and he might well be speaking out of turn by claiming to be beyond surprise.

He looked up, caught her staring raptly and automatically reached for his napkin to wipe his mouth. "What?"

"It's been said that olives are an aphrodisiac."

He choked, waved her away when she attempted to pound him on the back. Yep. Definitely spoke too soon. She'd surprised him. And charmed him right down to his boots.

"Tell me something, legs. You're bold, sexy and gorgeous, and you make the best fried chicken I've ever tasted—so how come some lucky guy hasn't caught you?"

She gave him another of those direct, disquieting looks filled with sensuality. "I'm trying hard to let you."

"Not by me. By a nice guy."

"Why do you do that?"

"What?"

"Think you're not a good guy."

"Didn't you think just that when you came here? Seems I recall something about you hanging around to see if I could sufficiently clean up my lifestyle before you'd entrust Katie to me."

She shrugged. "So I didn't know you."

"You still don't," he said softly.

"Then why won't you let me?"

"Legs, you don't know what you're getting into here. You're an innocent—"

"Stop right there." She held up her hand like a traffic cop. "I don't know why you insist on stereotyping me, or where you get the idea that I'm so pure and prim and proper. I'm not a virgin, you know— well, not exactly."

His hat lifted a good two inches as his brows shot up. "Well, don't hold back."

"I'm not. You're the one holding back."

He'd meant it rhetorically. Trust Dora to take his words at face value. "Just so we're straight here, maybe you ought to tell me what you mean by 'not exactly.'"

"I had a relationship in college, and we came very close to the actual consummation."

He choked on a swallow of pasta. "See? It's words like *that* that convince me I'm right and you're wrong here. You're an innocent, and I'm the big bad wolf. And because of that, neither one of us is going to go to Grandma's house!"

The maddening woman actually laughed at him. *Consummation* for crying out loud. If that didn't scream prim and proper he didn't know what did.

"The wolf didn't have sexual designs on Red Riding Hood."

"The hell he didn't. He was a wolf."

She chuckled again, then put her hand on his knee.

His gaze shot to his fly to see if his arousal was as blatantly obvious as it felt. He was dying here.

"Ethan?"

"What?"

"Would you look at me?"

"I'm looking, legs. That's the problem." Through the cotton of her snug tank top, the lacy outline of her bra teased his imagination.

"What do I have to do to let you know I'm human?" she asked. "I have flaws and...and desires just like the next woman."

He might have been able to resist if she'd been smiling. But the earnest entreaty in her lake-blue eyes would take a much stronger man than him to turn away.

He slipped his palm along her jaw, wrapped his fingers around the back of her neck and drew her closer. "I want to go on record as having said that I warned you."

She nodded. "It's recorded. Now shut up and kiss me."

"Yes, ma'am." He brushed her mouth with his, then took off his hat, tossed it aside and hooked a palm around her hip, dragging her closer.

This was insanity, but he couldn't help himself. She tasted of lemonade and smelled like wildflowers. She kissed like an innocent, yet still made his blood boil.

He shifted, eased her down on the blanket, followed her and angled her head for a deeper kiss. "Open for me."

Her eyelashes fanned upward as she gazed up at him with a look that was anything but innocent.

Before he realized what was happening, she threaded her fingers through his hair and kissed him with a fervor that suggested she did this for a living. And did it very well. Her full lips fit his perfectly.

Sheer surprise fogged his mind when she raised her hips, pressing against his pelvis. He could control himself, he rationalized. He could stop any time. He would just spend a few minutes more indulging in the sweet taste of her lips. Nothing more.

Her tongue swept an erotic circle around his, and he was lost. Overwhelmed with greed and lust, and forgetting completely every one of his reservations, he shifted his weight, kneed her legs apart and pressed his hard arousal right where he desperately wanted to bury himself.

She moaned, and the sound fueled him, had his hand racing over her side, up and down, raising the hem of her flirty tank top. At last, he filled his hand with the incredibly soft weight of her breast.

And felt her stiffen.

It was only a split-second, involuntary reaction due to inexperience, but it had the same effect as tipping an icy-cold trough of water over him. He came to his senses, remembered where they were.

"This isn't a good idea." Total understatement.

"Yes, it is." She still held him in the vee of her thighs, warm, moist heat radiating even through two layers of denim—his and hers. "I want to make love with you."

Ethan smoothed her top back in place and sat up. He was scared to death. That kiss stunned him like no other had and he told himself he ought to jump on his horse and run like crazy.

He'd never been with a virgin—even a "not exactly" one. His relationships had been mature and sophisticated, based on mutual desire with both parties knowing the rules.

Dora Watkins didn't know those rules. She'd never had sex—casual or otherwise.

Yet here she was, this beautiful, maddening, exciting woman innocently giving him the green light to make love to her. What was she thinking? Hell, what was *he* thinking?

"An innocent," he murmured, not really meaning to say it aloud. But despite that virtue, she packed a powerful kiss. One that would have spoken of experience if he hadn't known better.

She drew herself up beside him and, without warning, punched him right in the shoulder.

For a minute he was too stunned to speak. "What the heck was that for?"

"For being such a prude."

"Me?"

"Yes, you. And for making me feel..." She waved her hand, obviously unable to come up with the choice word she wanted. "You know."

He raised his brow, truly perplexed. "No."

"Inadequate," she finished.

Now *that* was an uncalled-for blow below the belt. He had a well-deserved reputation, and he'd never once left a woman unsatisfied.

"Are you saying that kiss didn't curl your toes? Because baby, if that's the case—"

"Of course it curled my toes, God bless it all. And I thought I was doing a fine job of curling yours, too, but obviously I'm deluding myself by thinking I have any such skills."

He was still hung up on her "God bless it all"—wondering if she meant it literally or if it was some clean way of swearing—and it was a moment or two before he finally looked closely enough to see the stricken look in her blue eyes. She thought she didn't turn him on.

"Ah, legs, you did too good a job." He lifted her right into his lap, held her there when she put up a bit of struggle. His lips caressed her temple, her hair. "I want you so bad I can't see straight, but I'm trying to be a good guy."

"Did I say I wanted a good guy?"

His lips curved against her hair. "As a matter of fact, you did."

"When?"

"Right after the auction, when you insisted you were moving in with me. You definitely maligned my life-style and my character."

He saw her lips twitch. "For Katie's benefit, not mine," she said, and scooted off his lap. She picked up her sketch pad and quickly, expertly patched together bold strokes and clever shading, and within seconds had a grinning, lecherous-looking wolf on one side of the page and a serene meadow and creek on the other.

Ethan chuckled, shook his head. "Uh-uh. We're not heating things up again, and we're not going to Grandma's house." Even if he did totally lose his mind and make love with her, it wouldn't be out here in the open with the baby sleeping next to them. For Dora's first time, she deserved a bed and a lock on the door and the privacy to spend all night.

But he wasn't going to give in. Preacher or not, her daddy would likely shoot him right between the eyes.

And besides the fact that Ethan was fairly partial to his face was the even more important fact that he'd never been with a virgin before. No sense in messing up his clean record now.

Chapter Eleven

By that evening, when the house was quiet and the day's work done, Ethan knew that his clean record was about to suffer, after all.

The glass of scotch and water that was halfway to his mouth slowly lowered, hitting the teak bar surface with a sharp click when Dora paused in the doorway of the den.

Desire, edgy and sharp, shot up the inside of his legs, all the way to his groin. She wore a flirty little slip dress. And wouldn't you know it, the silky, thin, barely-there garment was black.

Sultry, erotic, midnight-black.

How was a man supposed to stand up under this kind of pressure?

"You're doing that on purpose, aren't you?" he asked, shoving his hands in his pockets so he wouldn't reach out and take.

"Yes." Bold as you please, she stepped up to him, and placed her palm on his chest. "Your brothers are gone to town, Katie's asleep for the night."

Her hand slipped right over his heart. Had it moved

anyplace else, he might have been able to resist. He couldn't explain it, but somehow his heart seemed to be responding even more than his body.

"I want you to make love with me, Ethan. Teach me to make love to you."

He groaned. His hands came out of his pockets, but still he didn't touch. It took Herculean effort, but he was proud of his control. It seemed he had so little around Dora. "Why me?"

"Because you make me feel things I've never felt before. When I look at you, I can feel every place my heart beats. It's like a pulsing heat and it's driving me crazy."

Most women would not have openly admitted that, and because the bold words came from Dora, Ethan knew that his control had just bit the dust.

She wanted him to be the one to teach her, and Heaven help him, he wanted the same.

He'd already decided that had she been anyone else, they could have enjoyed a mature intimacy while they were under the same roof.

She was offering exactly what he wanted. What he was used to.

So why did this particular time seem so different? So special? Why did this time, with this woman, seem so vitally important?

He placed his hand at her throat, tipped her chin up with his thumb. "Be very sure, legs." His lips brushed hers, stoking the fire. "Because if we start this, I don't think I'll have the character, much less the ability, to stop."

She didn't even hesitate. "I'm sure, Ethan."

His lips slid to her throat, her shoulder, then back to her pouty lips. She arched against him and wrapped her arms around his neck, standing on the balls of her feet. The only barrier between them was a thin layer of silk and a straining panel of denim that was about to burst its seams.

When she snuggled her hips even harder against him, Ethan felt his gut erupt in fire. She kissed him like a woman who knew what she was doing, her mouth open, her tongue matching and mating with his.

If this was hell, he decided, he was happy to be here.

Nevertheless, in a fleeting moment of sanity, he reached up and gripped her wrists, bringing her arms down to her sides. "We should slow down."

"No, we shouldn't."

Her lips were swollen and glistening. With her arms down at her sides, the spaghetti straps of her siren dress slipped off her shoulders, the slinky material catching on the plump swell of her breast.

"You're not wearing a bra."

"I'm not wearing *any* underwear."

"Oh, man."

Dora gripped his hips to steady herself. She hadn't meant to blurt that out, had intended for him to find out on his own. But honestly, foreplay had never been this intense, making her pant and throb and want to climb right up his body.

She ran the tip of her tongue up and down his neck, lightly sucked the pulsing skin just above his collarbone.

In a move that left her whirling, he took her lip again, pulled the straps on her dress farther down her arms and walked her backward. Her hips hit the long marble-topped table behind the sofa.

He hooked his hands around the backs of her thighs and lifted her onto the table, then stepped between her legs. Her dress had already ridden up, but Ethan pushed it even higher as he slid his palms erotically up the sides of her legs and cupped her bottom, scooting her right up against him, pelvis to pelvis.

Dora wondered if she was going to hyperventilate. She couldn't seem to drag enough air into her lungs. And Ethan didn't seem much better off.

He went still, rested his forehead against hers. "I ought to be shot."

"Please, no. At least not until you finish this."

Laughter shook his shoulders. He leaned his upper body back, keeping his hands on her behind and their lower bodies intimately pressed, her silky dress hem gathered around her waist. "You are so refreshingly direct."

"Comes from being a tomboy." She gasped when his finger lightly, lazily stroked the swell of her breast, just above the material of her dress, back and forth, his gaze following the movement, then lifting back to hers.

"There's not a single thing tomboyish about you." He ran his hands up and down her arms, from her shoulders to the tips of her fingers, then treated her legs to the same erotically charged ministrations, taking his time as he stroked from her knees to the outde of her thighs, to her behind, then back down. "You have the softest skin."

Soft or not, she only knew that it was burning like white-hot fire where her naked, throbbing body pressed against the length of his arousal.

She wrapped her legs around his hips, tried desperately not to whimper. "I seem to be showing a lot more skin than you."

Without breaking contact, he crossed his arms, gripped the hem of his T-shirt and pulled it over his head. "Better?"

Dora was without words or voice as she placed her hands on his glorious chest, treated his taut skin to the same up and down motion as he'd done to her, mapping his masculine contours.

She brushed his nipples, heard him draw in a swift breath, saw chill bumps raise across his chest.

"Is that wrong?"

"No." His jaw clenched, and a vein rose along his neck as though he was straining. "It's very right." He took her wrists and lowered her hands, planting them against the tabletop. "But this is your first time, and since you've entrusted your body to me, we'll play by my rules."

"And those are?"

"No touching, on your part, for a while."

"I don't know if I can—" She gasped as he tilted her head to the side and gave her a kiss that rippled clear to her soul.

"Yes, you can." Ethan kissed her throat, her earlobe, then slid his lips over her neck and shoulder, felt her squirm. The movement nearly sent him over the edge. He was torturing himself, but he was determined to take it slow, to turn her mindless with pleasure, to ensure that when he was finally inside her, her body would be ready to accept him, to guarantee her first experience at making love would be unforgettably etched in her memory.

She smelled of wildflowers and tasted like a dream. He wanted to touch her all over, faster, harder…more. But he held back, kept his touch slow and firm, determined to drench her in pleasure. From the moment she'd walked into his life, she'd kept him off balance, thrusting him into situations that made him feel hapless.

Here, though, they were in his arena. He held the reins. And the knowledge sent his ego soaring.

Ethan heard her whimper when he pressed his thumbs to the top of her pubic bone. Watching her, still using only his thumbs, he combed through her curls and downward to the slick heat of her.

She cried out and arched against him, and he nearly lost it right then and there. The top of her dress fell to her waist and she tried to lift her hands, but the straps trapping her arms prevented it.

"You are so beautiful," he said, awed. Her breasts were considerably more than a handful. He cupped their weight, ran his thumbs over the hard tips. "So beautiful."

Until tonight, she'd worn a bra beneath her clothes. Admittedly, it had been fairly visible beneath several of those tank tops she favored, but visible or not, it had been hiding intoxicatingly voluptuous breasts.

So perfect. Guaranteed to make a man beg.

Dora Watkins had a body made for lovemaking.

"We need a bed. Hold your legs tight around me." He pulled the straps of her dress all the way down, then slipped his hands beneath her bottom and lifted her. Her arms came around his neck, those remarkably soft breasts pillowed against his chest, creating a fiery friction with each step he took, testing his control as it had never been tested.

"I do like those long legs of yours, darlin'." She wasn't much bigger than a minute and weighed even less.

"I figured that out the first time you ogled them."

"I didn't ogle." In his bedroom he flicked on the lamp, holding her easily with one arm, then took his wallet from his hip pocket and tossed it on the nightstand. He put a knee on the mattress and laid her down. Without breaking contact, he followed, fitting himself between her legs, torturing himself as he pressed his arousal against her. He hadn't yet taken off his jeans, which was a good thing. Hopefully, if he kept his body imprisoned, he wouldn't rush.

It might make him crazy, but he promised himself he'd take his time, get it right. Because suddenly the most important thing in the world to him was getting it right. He couldn't remember ever feeling this way before—probably because he'd never been entrusted with a woman's most cherished gift. And though he might not deserve that gift, he was going to treasure it.

He threaded his fingers through the hair at her temples, gazed down at her. Her eyes skittered away, and that wasn't like her. "What?" he asked softly.

She shrugged. "I'm...I don't know."

"Afraid?"

"Yes." She sighed. "And I hate admitting that."

He pressed his lips lightly to her eyelids, her cheeks, the corner of her mouth. "Do you want to stop?"

"No."

"If it makes you feel better, I'm scared, too."

"You are not."

"Yes. I don't want to hurt you. And I don't want to scare you. But I'm afraid I'll do both."

She wrapped her arms around him, buried her face in his neck. "I think I'm more apprehensive than scared. I've never been naked in front of a man before."

He raised his upper body and his brows at the same time. "What about art class?"

"That was different. It wasn't..."

"Sexual?" He slid down, traced his lips over the swell of her breasts. "Arousing?" He shifted to his side, lifted the soft weight of her breast in his hand. Her dress was merely a silky band bunched around her waist. He kept his thigh over her lower body, giving her time to adjust to his gaze, to his touch.

She sucked in a breath when his thumb stroked her nipple.

"Do you like that?"

Dora didn't know if she could find her voice. Her heart was pumping so hard she wondered that it wasn't visible. "Yes." A whisper. She touched his bare chest, reveling in the smooth skin and firm muscles.

He gently circled her wrists and drew her hands away from him, pinning them to the mattress. Linking his fingers with hers, he kissed her long and hard, sweeping nearly every coherent thought from her head. "No touching, remember?" he said.

"But I want to know what gives you pleasure, too."

He ran his hand down the underside of her arm, moved his leg from across her thighs and swept a path of fire down her side, from her chest to her knees and back up again.

"Next time. This time I'm going to show you what your body can feel. All for you. Just your pleasure."

Oh, that sounded so selfish, and she might have told him so if his hand hadn't smoothed straight up the inside of her thigh and cupped her like no man ever had.

Hot desire and love rushed through her veins, right to her heart, and then pulsed between her legs. This is what she'd waited for these last twenty-seven years. Just this. Ethan. His touch. His taste.

His fingers didn't linger long in any one spot and Dora wanted to scream. Each touch was different, yet they all pulled the same taut, incredibly arousing strings in her body, raising desire to a fever pitch. The rush of emotions was almost too much. She tried to focus, found she couldn't.

And all the while he watched her, seemed to be gauging her response as he molded her body and emotions to his will with skill and style.

"Lift up," he coached.

As she dug her heels into the mattress and lifted

her hips, he slid her little slip dress all the way off, leaving her bare to his gaze.

"You take my breath away." His voice was raw and reverent.

"Likewise," she said with a nervous chuckle that came out more like a pant. Turning on her side, she pressed into him, attempting to shield herself from his hot, intense eyes. She suddenly felt shy and needed a moment of respite.

The erotic feel of denim against her bare skin inflamed. She wanted to feel all of him against her, but at the same time the barrier of his pants meant that nothing would happen too soon. She appreciated his thoughtfulness, knew his intention was to take his time with her, ease her into the initiation of lovemaking, yet she wanted to tell him it wasn't necessary.

With his hand on her hip, he pressed her back against the mattress. "I could almost be satisfied just looking at you."

The reverent way he said the words, the incredibly exquisite way his gaze skimmed over her, banished the last of her apprehension. He made her feel beautiful, secure, cherished.

He was the man she loved, the man she'd entrusted with her virginity.

"Almost," he repeated, then using the unfair advantage of his experience, he skillfully employed lips, tongue, hands and his whole body to set her on fire, to send her on an erotic journey that she knew without a doubt she'd never forget.

Sensation sharpened, nearly became surreal. The room faded away, and there was only the bed and the two of them. Outside, a barn owl hooted, and a coyote yipped. But inside, there was only touch and taste and feel. He found pleasure points she never imagined she had—the back of her knees, the underside of her breasts, the side of her neck. When his lips closed over the sensitive skin just beneath her ear she shifted restlessly. When he lightly sucked the skin into his mouth, she moaned.

"That's it, baby. Tell me what feels good."

"All of it." She sucked in a breath when his finger slipped inside her. "Oh!" Colors exploded behind her closed eyelids. She'd told him she'd engaged in everything except actual consummation. She'd been terribly wrong.

She'd never felt anything like the flex of Ethan's fingers inside her body. She wasn't sure she could survive this much pleasure.

Her hips shifted, seeking contact. She needed...oh, she didn't know *what* she needed. "Please."

"Not yet." He withdrew his hand, and she nearly wept. "Shh." Firmer now, faster, his palms smoothed up and down her body, from her neck to her toes and every erotic point in between.

"At least take off your pants," she said with what little breath she had.

Instead of obliging, he grabbed her hips and pulled her tight against his pelvis, holding her there, breathing heavily, his fingers flexing against her behind. "I need a minute."

"I don't have a minute, Ethan. I feel like I'm going to come apart."

He glanced down at her, gave her one of those

incredibly tender, incredibly intense looks. "I *mean* for you to come apart," he said softly, and rose to remove his pants and take a condom out of his wallet.

For a moment he stood beside the bed, gloriously naked. He had a body that should have been displayed on a calendar—or on a statue in a fine arts museum.

Her eyes widened only slightly when her gaze slid down to take in all of him.

He smiled and eased back on the bed, gathered her in his arms. "We'll fit," he assured.

She wasn't certain about that, but at the moment she didn't care, because his clever hands were once more sweeping over her body, caressing, squeezing, stroking, bringing her just to the edge of something incredible, then starting all over again. Patiently. Thoroughly.

Dora thought she'd go mad.

She clamped her hands on his shoulders, tried to pull him on top of her. "Ethan..."

"I know." He shifted between her thighs, positioned himself over her. With one hand against the mattress to steady his weight, he swept the other beneath her hips, and lifted.

"Hold on to me now." His voice was gritty and strained.

She felt him press against her, intimately, hard and fiery hot. She held her breath as he slowly entered her, just a bit, then withdrew.

She whimpered, was about to beg when he pushed forward again.

It wasn't enough. "Ethan..."

"Shh, sweetheart." His lips brushed her temple, his breath ragged in her ear. "Just hold on."

In and out he moved, slowly, erotically, each time pressing a bit harder, tipping her hips a bit farther. He moved his hand around between them, lightly circled his thumb around the most sensitive part of her body, and Dora came apart, barely aware that at that exact moment he'd thrust completely into her.

Her body pulsed around him, streaking up to another crest, stunning her with the speed and intensity of what could only be described as pure rapturous bliss. Her heart beat so hard, she wondered how a person could do this without having a heart attack.

"Okay?" Ethan asked, his lips sketching her cheeks, her ear, the corner of her eye.

"More than okay. I feel—"

He put a finger over her lips. "If you go into detail, this'll all be over in a minute." A bead of sweat rolled down his temple. "I was hoping for a bit longer than that."

She smiled, smoothed her hands down his broad back and over the mounds of his firm butt. "You can move now."

"Sure? I'm not hurting you?"

She shook her head, squeezed his behind and pulled him deeper inside her. "Show me, Ethan. Make love to me."

Ethan gently kissed her lips, then holding her gaze with his, he began to move, in and out, slowly, his control hanging on by a bare thread as he felt each inch of his body sinking into hers, felt the warmth of her femininity pulsate around him, grip him, hold him.

Had it ever felt this right? Had there ever been such a tight perfect fit? His body was screaming for release, but his head was sending a completely different message. Hold on. Draw it out. Savor. Feel. Just feel. Make it good for her. For Dora. His Dora.

A possessiveness he didn't understand swept through his blood as he thrust harder and faster. Reaching for the back of her thighs, he drew her legs up, wrapped them around his waist, heard her muffle a scream against the side of his neck.

"That's it, baby. Again." She'd already climaxed several times. He wanted more. He wanted it all.

His mind hazed when she sobbed his name, when she matched his moves, his rhythm, and with innocence and sheer abandon pushed them both over the edge of blissful madness.

WHEN ETHAN WAS ABLE to think again, he looked quickly down at Dora. "Are you okay? Did I hurt you?" He called himself every kind of fool for losing control that way.

He shifted to his side, brushed the damp bangs off her forehead, placed a kiss to the skin he'd uncovered. An apology.

"Ethan, I'm more than fine." Dora rolled with him, not yet ready to give up the contact of their bodies. She was satisfied, there was no doubt about it. But still she craved more.

Not knowing if that was normal, if perhaps he'd released some hidden nymphomaniac inside her, she concentrated on bringing her breathing back under control, concentrated on sophistication.

"What's that look, legs?"

"What look?"

Incredibly, he hooked a leg over and around the back of hers and in one impressively fluid movement, he sat up, taking her with him. Before she could even draw a breath, he was sitting cross-legged on the bed and she was straddling his lap.

The intimate contact the position afforded made her moan.

He cupped her bottom, pulled her more snugly against him.

"What's going through that gorgeous head of yours?"

She shook her head.

"Are you sorry?"

"Oh, no. That's not it at all. It's just that…" She shrugged, the words right there aching to come out. Oh, what the heck. "I want to do it again."

His smile tilted just at the corner of his mouth, lifted slowly. "I didn't get it right the first time?"

She hooked her arms around his neck, brushed the tips of her breasts against his chest. He was teasing her, and she could give it right back.

"You got it very right, cowboy. I now know what it feels like to be made love to. And very well, I might add."

"Mmm." He ducked his head and kissed the underside of her jaw. "A performance rating. I like that."

It took a minute to remember her train of thought

because his lips were now doing something breath-takingly clever to her ear.

"Wait." She put a hand on his chest, gave a gentle shove.

His gaze lifted, his blue eyes filled with a desire so intense Dora could only stare.

I love you. The urge to say the words was so strong her throat ached with the effort to hold them back. He wasn't ready to hear that declaration just yet. She didn't know if he ever would be, but she could hope. For now, though, there was a different agenda.

"You've made love to me. Now I want to know the flip side. I want to know how to make love to *you.*"

"I think we can manage that." His voice was no longer teasing. His body began to swell against her.

"I don't sound too...needy or anything?"

"Needy is good. Especially, uh, in this particular context."

"In that case..." She scooted back in his lap just far enough to reach between them and take him in her hand.

His breath drew in swiftly.

She raised her eyes to his. "Teach me," she whispered.

He put his hand over hers, showing her exactly what he liked.

"Ethan?"

"Mmm, baby, that's so good."

She reveled in his praise and in the different textures of his body. "This won't be the end of it, you know. Once I learn how to make love *to* you, I imagine it'll be necessary to have a quiz.''

''Definitely necessary,'' he said against her jaw. He guided her hand over him, clenching his teeth as his body grew incredibly hot and hard.

''Man alive, Dora, I don't have an ounce of control around you.''

He released her hand, snatched open the nightstand drawer and took out the whole box of condoms, hoping they weren't expired.

He'd never brought a woman home to his bedroom. Never wanted the memories of one left in this room.

Now he couldn't wait to *make* memories.

''You think that'll be enough?''

He chuckled against her lips. ''I'm crazy about you, legs.''

''Mmm, I'm pretty crazy about you, too.''

''If I've died and gone to Heaven, don't tell me, okay?''

''Okay. At least not for the next little while. Because I need you well and truly alive if you're going to complete my education.''

''Why do I feel as if I'm the one who'll get the education?'' And that was the end of the conversation, Ethan thought, because her untutored hands were driving him wild.

Next time, he decided. Next time he'd teach her how to torture his body.

Right now he had other designs on Dora Watkins.

Chapter Twelve

Ethan stood in the doorway of Katie's room and deliberately rapped his knuckles against the wall. The baby wiggled, but didn't wake. He sighed, feeling antsy. Katie was a late sleeper, making it difficult for him to jump right into morning chores.

He stepped back and glanced over the upstairs railing to the bottom of the stairs where Dora streaked by on her way back into the laundry room she'd converted into a dark room.

She hadn't been in bed when he'd woken. He'd prepared himself to deal with shy regrets. He should have known better than to think anything about Dora Watkins was shy.

Instead, she'd greeted him over coffee with a chirpy "hi" and an absent kiss that had landed somewhere between his cheek and his mouth—as though he was her *brother*, for crying out loud, and not the man she'd had hot sex with just hours before.

And now, here she was, flitting about as usual, acting as if she was the sophisticated one experienced in no-strings mornings after.

...nd Ethan was the one mooning like a lovesick ...lf.

Annoyed, he went back into Katie's room, prepared to shake the crib if necessary.

It wasn't necessary. She stood, holding on to the side railing of the oak baby bed, eight little teeth gleaming as she grinned and bobbed up and down on pudgy legs.

Everything within Ethan went soft with love.

"Hey, there, sweetheart. Promise me you'll always wake up with a smile just like that." He stepped up next to her, gently cupped her tiny head in his big hand, marveling at the contrast. "Except you need to wake up a little earlier. Can't be a lay-about on a ranch."

She danced some more and joyfully beat a stuffed rabbit against the railing.

"I know. You want out of the pen. No sense in killing the floppy ears." He lifted her up, and from previous experience he knew better than to hold her too close. Kissing her warm cheek, he carried her to the changing table and grabbed a fresh diaper.

"Let's change you and eat so we can get busy, okay?" He was becoming much more proficient at diapering, especially when she refrained from doing her wiggly worm impression. "Everybody else is already hard at work. If you're going to keep sleeping so late, we'll have to figure out a rotating shift. You've got two perfectly able uncles who could take turns getting you up."

He sat her up and pulled a T-shirt with a sunny duck swimming on its front over her head and couldn't help dropping a kiss on her sweet forehead when she blinked up at him. "And it wouldn't hurt Dora to take a turn or two, don't you think?"

"Doda," Katie babbled.

"Hey, was that a Daddy or Dora?" Instead of answering—he'd have fallen over if she had—she clapped him on the cheeks, then switched moods like lightning and gave him a bit of grief as he tried to thread her fat little feet through the legs of a pair of stretch pants.

By the time he'd accomplished the task, he was sweating and Katie's sunny smile had turned to testy grunts that would soon be full-blown screams if he didn't change the scenery in a hurry.

He swung her up in his arms and headed downstairs toward the kitchen, wondering if he should start interviewing baby-sitters. It made his heart stutter to think about Dora not being here forever, but it was a fact he'd have to face sooner or later.

It seemed she was easing back from Katie—both to temper the pain of her own departure, he imagined, as well as to make sure he was equipped with the proper skills to get along alone with Katie.

Alone until she was twenty-one, he realized suddenly. Alone when a string of pimply faced adolescent boys came around wanting to hang out with her...and more.

"Oh, man," he groaned.

"What?" Dora asked from behind him.

He whirled around, and although Katie obviously thought it was some new and fun game, Ethan's heart was actually thudding.

For crying out loud, he thought, disgusted with himself.

"Dating," he said. "I was thinking about dating."

"You?"

"No. Katie."

Dora grinned. "She's a bit young yet, don't you think?"

"Yes, but she won't always be young. And that means boys." He shuddered.

"Might not be such a problem. The only little boy I've seen so far is Hannah's son, Ian. Of course, that might work. There's only three years difference in their ages."

Ethan shook his head. "Ian's promised to Nikki."

"Excuse me?"

"Stony Stratton's little girl. I think they've worked out dowries and everything."

Dora giggled. "Well then, you'll likely have no worries."

"I will if Ozzie and his cohorts get their way and manage to fill Shotgun Ridge with women and babies."

"There is that."

Dora started to walk out of the room, but Ethan caught her hand. "What's the rush?"

"Uh…I've got work."

"Don't we all." He tugged, bringing her closer, his gaze fastened on her mouth as though pulled by a magnet. "Stay for a bit? Keep me company?"

She looked from him to Katie and back. "Are you crying uncle?"

"No, but I thought about that this morning. There's

no reason why Grant and Clay can't rotate with me over the morning shift with Katie.''

Her blond brows rose. ''Have you discussed this with them?''

''Not yet. But I know they'll agree. It'll be better than leaving her with a baby-sitter all day.''

The reminder that Dora wouldn't be here indefinitely hung heavy in the air. He wanted to talk to her about it but didn't know how.

He wasn't offering anything beyond the moment. And she deserved so much better.

Instead of sitting, she gave his hand a squeeze, then stunned him by raising his knuckles to her lips and pressing a gentle kiss to the rough skin.

An ache filled his chest and he didn't know why. With an unreadable look that scared him on several levels, she smiled and stepped back. ''I really do need to get some work done. I've spent so much time taking photographs, I've neglected doing the actual sketches. And those are what pay the bills.''

An eerie desperation came over Ethan, settling like a fist behind his sternum. He wasn't ready to give her up just yet.

''Spend the afternoon with me,'' he blurted. ''I mean, if you think you'll have your sketches done by then.''

She smiled. ''I won't have them done, but I'll have made good progress. What did you have in mind?''

''A surprise. I'll arrange it.''

AFTER CALLING IRIS BREWER, who said she'd be thrilled to mind Katie for the afternoon, Ethan drove into town, his truck filled with toys and clothes and diapers and everything else he could think of that Katie might need.

Traffic down Main Street was heavier than he'd expected. He looked around, noted the changes. The widows Bagley had spruced up their white clapboard with pots of colorful flowers and were serving refreshments to several women on the shaded porch. A No Vacancy sign hung out front. When had Mildred and Opal had vacancies to begin with? Ethan wondered.

He waved to the sheriff, Cheyenne Bodine, who stood on the sidewalk in front of the jail talking to Ozzie, Henry and another man Ethan didn't recognize. A fairly new Chevy pickup with McCall Developers & General Contractors painted on the door was parked in the diagonal space in front of the sheriff's office.

Progress, Ethan thought. Evidently the geezers' plans were paying off after all. Homes turned into boarding houses, and enough cars on Main Street to require a slower speed and a sharper eye than normal. In light of these changes, there might be room for a bit more developing around town. He would have to find out what was going on.

Turning off Main street, he wound through several blocks of tidy houses with velvety green lawns kept vibrant and thriving by Rainbirds chugging back and forth, drenching the ground with moisture.

Iris and Lloyd Brewer's home was on a corner lot. Nicely trimmed hedges and beds overflowing with colorful flowers gave the modest two-story a welcoming warmth.

Once he got Katie out of her seat and had loaded bags and straps over his shoulders like a pack horse, he made his way to the front porch, where Iris waited with the screen door open.

"Land sakes, Ethan. Did you bring the entire house?"

"Seems like it." He bent to kiss Iris's cheek, and the diaper bag and a satchel slipped off his shoulder and fell to the gleaming wood floor with a thunk. "I didn't know if you had any toys so I brought some of hers. She's good about entertaining herself—most of the time. I don't want to scare you off from baby-sitting—"

"Ethan?"

He grinned. "I know. I'm a nervous wreck." He couldn't remember ever admitting to such a state—or if he'd actually ever felt it before. "This is my first time leaving her with somebody else."

"She'll be fine. Won't you, lamb?" Iris held out her hands, and Katie happily leaned into them. "Oh, I never thought my arms would hold so many honorary grandbabies."

Ethan didn't say anything. Timmy Malone had been Iris's grandson and Ethan's godson. They both felt the loss.

"Just put her things over there on the sofa, Ethan."

"Should I get the car seat out of the truck in case you want to go somewhere?"

"I've got my own now. What with Ian and then the new baby due in a couple of months, I figured I needed one. I tell you, Ethan, for once I'm actually pleased with Lloyd and the other old goats' meddling.''

Ethan set a wind-up bumblebee on the floor along with several other toys. ''You guard Katie around those geezers,'' he admonished teasingly. ''They'll have her corrupted in no time.''

Iris laughed. ''You have my word.''

''Okay. I think that's it. We should be back by early evening. Is that okay?''

''Why don't you just leave her here overnight? You've obviously brought enough provisions. Lloyd and I'll take her to church in the morning and you can collect her then.''

''I don't know…'' It was tough enough leaving her here for the afternoon. He was so attached to this little girl, it worried him to leave her overnight.

''Really, Ethan. It'll be much easier. And we'd love to have her.''

Ethan nodded. ''Thanks, Iris.''

DORA WAITED FOR ETHAN by the hangar. She had no idea if she was dressed properly for wherever they were going. She wore a sleeveless, tank-style white bodysuit, a pair of pleated sand-colored shorts and sandals. Just to be on the safe side, she'd dropped a pair of sneakers into her oversize tote bag that held everything from last year's toothpicks and crumpled tissue to her sketch pad and pencils.

She turned and shaded her eyes as Ethan's truck came up the concrete driveway. Through white fences, mares and foals lifted elegant heads and watched him pass.

Instead of stopping the truck at the garage, he continued on around to the hangar.

Dora felt her heart skip with a thrill, and she cautioned herself to take it easy. His tobacco-colored hat nearly brushed the roof of the cab. He had an elbow propped out the open window, a hand lazily draped over the steering wheel...and an empty baby seat riding next to him.

For one ridiculously insane moment, Dora felt tears sting her throat and eyes. Despite how incredibly sexy it looked for a big, tough cowboy to sport a baby seat in his pickup, the fact that the seat was empty gave her a punch.

It reminded her that she could very well be leaving with an empty baby seat herself.

She drew in a breath, shook off the panic, told herself she still had time.

Time to make Ethan fall in love with her, time for him to ask her to stay.

He pulled the truck to a stop a few feet away from her, got out and simply stood there on the running board. With his folded arms resting on top of the open door, he gazed at her with a sexy intensity that made her want to tug at the scoop neck of her bodysuit.

The man was handsome as sin, and as temptations went, Dora was more than willing to have another taste of the forbidden.

When his eyes gave her another slow once-over, nerves crowded in her throat, fluttered in her stomach. "What?"

"You look incredible."

She smothered a giggle, her head rushing. "Let's don't get carried away." It was just shorts and a top, for goodness' sake. Still, her breath caught and held when he shut the truck's door and slowly, purposefully came toward her with a loose-hipped stride that screamed sensuality.

She'd never had anyone look at her with such utter intent—sexual intent. Her chest lifted and fell when at last she remembered to breathe.

He stopped in front of her, the corner of his mouth tipped up in the barest hint of a smile. An expression that made her tremble.

"I was right. You look incredible." His knuckles brushed her cheek, then the skin just above the low scoop of her top. "So soft and warm."

Dora blinked and swallowed hard. "Are we staying in or leaving?" Given a choice, she'd just as soon head back to the house. He was making her hot...and needy. Wondrous desire was springing like a well inside her.

He smiled, gently wrapped his fingers around her neck and tipped her chin up with his thumb. "Depends. How are you feeling after last night?"

Did he mean mentally or physically? "Uh... wonderful, thank you."

His smile grew. "Are you sore?"

Oh. Physically. "Um, no." A bit. She didn't know why this conversation was flustering her so. It was exactly the kind of exchange her brothers might have engaged her in. Not about being sore over sex, of course—but a provocative exchange of words to see if they could get a rise out of her. She took a deep breath, looked him square in the eye. "Are *you?*"

He threw back his head and laughed. "Man, I'm crazy about you."

Her heart leaped, but she couldn't allow herself to put too much emphasis on his declaration. Crazy and in love were two entirely different animals.

Weren't they?

He looped his arm around her shoulders and led her around behind the hangar where a helicopter rested on a cement pad.

"More big-boy toys, I see."

"Isn't it great? It's a Bell Ranger. Older model, but it's a hot dog."

"Just like the pilot," she mused. "Are you trying to impress me?"

"Yes." He grinned down at her. "Is it working?"

She shrugged, tried hard to keep a straight face. "I'll admit, I've never ridden in a helicopter. Now a Lear jet's a different matter."

"Dora, Dora." He shook his head and tisked. "I keep forgetting you've got Quentin Watkins's oil money coming out of your ears. At least let me pretend for a while."

She winked, and just to please herself, because she couldn't stand it another minute, she went up on tiptoe, wrapped her arms around his neck and kissed him.

He reacted immediately. His hands swiftly came up her sides, settled beneath her armpits, nearly lifting her off her toes, then swept back down. Before she could think, he had his leg wedged between hers and his hands on her butt, tilting her hard against his arousal. The kiss went from impulsive to frenzied in mere seconds.

A discreet cough had them tearing apart like guilty children caught playing doctor behind the barn.

Grant leaned against the side of the hangar, booted ankles crossed, his chocolate-brown hat tipped back.

Dora felt her face flame and couldn't quite meet his gaze.

Ethan didn't have any such problem. He scowled without repentance.

"Just thought I'd come around and see if anybody was interested in thanking me for hauling the Ranger out of the hangar for them." Grant straightened from against the wall and tugged his hat. "But since you appear to be, uh…otherwise engaged, I'll leave you to it."

"You could have left us to it without interrupting," Ethan said tersely.

"Yes, I imagine I could have. Wouldn't have been nearly as entertaining, though." He nodded toward the helicopter. "Be good, you two."

Ethan was still scowling even after his brother had walked away. "That's the problem with living with your brothers. No privacy. And no respect. Sorry."

"You're apologizing to me? The girl with four ornery brothers? Besides, I started it."

His gazed dropped to her mouth. "That you did, legs." He opened the passenger door of the helicopter. "Your chariot, ma'am."

After they were buckled in, he spent several

minutes doing a preflight check and messing with all kinds of gadgets.

When he fired up the engine and the rotors started turning with a high whine, whipping faster and faster, becoming louder with each revolution, Dora felt a giddy thrill shoot through her veins. She wasn't afraid of flying, but a helicopter was an untried experience. Still, the thought of the adventure made her tremble just a bit.

Through the headphones, she heard Ethan's voice. "Ready?"

She looked over at him and grinned. "Absolutely."

For a moment it was almost as though he couldn't look away, as though he found her the most interesting, irresistible person on the planet. And while she might well be reading entirely too much into a look, it felt nice, anyway.

The whoop of the rotors beat the wind with deep thumps and the engine whined, pitching higher as it revved.

"Oh!" Dora exclaimed softly as the tail lifted, then the front. They flew forward and rose into a turn, the nose of the chopper still angled down, making Dora feel as though she should brace her hands on the dash or something.

She glanced at Ethan, emotions zinging through her faster than she could keep up. He wore dark aviation sunglasses and a headset with a little microphone that nearly touched his sculpted lips. He looked sexy and capable, his hands working the controls of the chopper with assurance and skill. A Western-cut shirt with snaps up the front hugged his broad shoulders and tapered waist and was tucked into ice-blue denim that molded his hips and thighs in a manner that had Dora's eyes darting away.

If she didn't stop fantasizing about his body, it was going to be a long, uncomfortable flight. Which reminded her, she had no idea how long a trip this was.

"Where are we going?" She spoke into the headset, familiar with they way they worked.

"I told you, it's a surprise."

"Can you give me a hint how long it'll take to get there?"

"Not long."

Happy to let herself be surprised, and trusting Ethan fully, Dora looked out the wraparound window at the countryside. They were flying toward a mountainous ridge, dense with pines and other evergreens. The beauty of Montana was diverse and breathtaking. The flat prairies had an appeal all their own, but the parts that were richer in foliage and grassy hills were an absolute serenity feast for the eyes.

A comfortable silence settled over them as they scooted along at a fast clip. Dora was content just to relax in her seat and let the artist within her absorb the different colors and shapes and textures all around them.

Ethan pointed out sights and occasionally dipped the helicopter gently so Dora could get a better look. She laughed with joy as they skimmed the tops of giant cedars and Douglas fir, then gasped in wonder as a grotto-like clearing appeared beneath them.

"My gosh! It's so beautiful it takes my breath away." As they hovered in the helicopter, Dora gazed at the waterfall gently cascading into a midnight lagoon surrounded by smooth, moss-covered rocks and feathery ferns. A hidden paradise.

"I own it."

Her gaze whipped to his. "Get out."

His smile was slow and sexy as he nodded. Although his attention was focused on her, he was fully aware and in control of the Ranger.

"Okay, legs, admit it."

She nearly rolled her eyes and had a really hard time keeping a straight face. It was getting harder by the minute to resist anything about Ethan Callahan. "I'm not admitting a thing. Your ego won't be able to fit out the door of the helicopter."

He wrapped his fingers around the back of her neck, pulled her closer. "I can make you."

She wasn't absolutely certain she could speak. She gave it a try, anyway. "I'm sure you can. But then who's going to fly us?" The aircraft was holding steady, but still...

He cocked a sexy brow as if to say they had all day and he was perfectly happy to wait.

"Oh, all right." Although she felt a bubble of laughter tickle her throat, she pretended to be put out. "I'm impressed. I've never known anybody who owned a waterfall."

"And mineral springs."

"Mineral springs? Ethan, you own your own private spa! Land this thing, would you?"

"As you wish."

She nearly whacked him for teasing her, but a momentary shiver of apprehension tried to get its claws in her as they began dropping straight down. The landings she was used to were at a gradual descent.

She craned her neck to see what was below the chopper, relieved that there was a fairly large carpet of grass. The skids touched the ground with a gentle one-two bump, and then the whine of the rotor was winding down, whipping slower and slower until it finally stopped.

When Ethan unbuckled his seat belt and reached for the door handle, that was Dora's cue. She opened her own door and hopped down, drinking in the ambiance of the grotto. Kicking off her sandals, she turned in a wide circle, felt the cool blades of grass under her feet, heard the tumble of the waterfall and inhaled the sultry, sulfur scent of the hot springs.

Ethan leaned against the nose of the Ranger and watched her. Sometimes, just watching Dora was enough. She drank in life and experiences with such verve and awe.

She looked at him with a sunny smile, and he pushed away from the helicopter and held out his hand for her. She snuggled right under his arm, fitting perfectly. As though she'd always been there. As though that's where she would always belong.

He stopped at the edge of the spring. To the left, a cascade of snowmelt wound its way down the mountainside, sliding over rocks fuzzy with verdant moss, then emptied into the springs, keeping the sulfurous water at a pleasant temperature. A spot where the earth's skin was thin, not unlike Yellowstone a couple of hundred miles away.

Ethan pulled off his boots and socks so the warm water could lap at his toes.

"How many people know about this place?"

He shrugged. "Not many. There are no trails leading in. The only access is by air—unless you wanted to rappel down the face of the mountain."

In a move that was easy and felt right, Dora put her arms around his waist and laid her head on his chest. They stood just like that for several minutes, until Ethan could no longer ignore the soft press of her breasts against his side.

"Want to go in?"

"I didn't bring a suit."

He reached behind him and grabbed a handful of his T-shirt and tugged it over his head, then reached for the snap of his jeans. "Who needs a suit?"

"I'm not going skinny-dipping right out here in the open."

Something in his chest fluttered. Dora Watkins could boss and sass, and she could be as shy as a virgin...which she no longer was, thanks to him. But he wasn't going to get sidetracked by that right now.

"Getting modest on me, legs?" He shucked his pants, then hooked his fingers in the waistband of Dora's shorts, unzipped them and had them down her legs and off before she could blink.

But Ethan blinked. Her white bodysuit looked like a sexy one-piece bathing suit and fit like a second skin. Cut high at the legs it flowed over her contours and hugged her breasts like an erotic picture. He suddenly had an urge to see her wet, watch the material turn clear with the lap of water.

"Nice," he said roughly, tracing the edge of her collarbone, then down to the scoop neck of the top. "Sexy."

He lowered his mouth to hers, drank in her taste, felt the instant kick of desire that he'd never experienced with any other woman. What was it with Dora? What was so different? "You've put a spell on me, I think," he murmured.

"Mmm. I'm not into that."

"Are you into waterfalls and hot springs?"

She nibbled at his lips, his jaw, her tongue tracing a clever pattern over his neck. "Absolutely."

He slipped one shoulder of her top down her arm. "Dressed or not?"

"Not. I didn't bring a change of clothes and I'm not crazy about wet bodysuits."

"Mmm. I'd have liked to have seen it wet."

"Well, if you want to loan me your shirt, I imagine we could do a private wet T-shirt thing."

He peeled the bodysuit over her shoulders and down until she stepped out of it, taking the opportunity to kiss and lick his way back up her body. When he reached her mouth, her breath was coming in pants. "Maybe later. Ever made love under a waterfall?"

She shook her head.

He lifted her. "Wrap your legs around me."

Naked, he walked with her into the warm, silky pool of water, having trouble with his concentration as her breasts pressed erotically against his chest and her thighs hugged him like a boa. Their bodies brushed with each buoyant step.

"How many women have you brought here?" Although most would consider that question prying, there wasn't an ounce of apology in her tone.

"You're the first." The realization both surprised and troubled him. This had been his own private oasis. He'd never wanted the intrusion or the memories of another woman here. He hadn't even given that a thought when he'd brought Dora here.

"Good," she said.

"Just like that? You believe me?"

"Of course." Her voice was soft, her blue eyes serious.

Surrounded by giant cedars, feathery ferns and vibrant wild roses, she wrapped her arms around him and held him tight, held him as though he was the most important man in the world. It was a trust that humbled him. A trust he didn't know if he deserved.

He now realized that it wasn't her purity or who her daddy was that had made him resist being close. He'd been resisting because he didn't think he was good enough.

But right now, he couldn't find the energy or the strength to care whether or not he was what she needed. She'd given him the go-ahead for intimacy. And that freed him to take her places, to spend time with her, to make love with her. To enjoy her and revere her the way a man should enjoy and revere a woman.

For as long as she was here.

Dora wrapped her legs tighter around Ethan's waist, felt the warm, silky water lap at her waist and the underside of her breasts. She felt the fine tension in his shoulders and wondered at it. It was almost as though he had regrets.

Determined to banish those regrets, she poured everything she had into a soul-searing kiss that threatened to send her over the edge way too soon.

Breathing heavily, she forced herself to slow down. His hands were everywhere at once, rubbing her back, her sides, cupping the weight of her breasts. He leaned against a smooth rock, propped her with his thigh, exerted just enough pressure to make her whimper.

His lips sipped water from her jaw, beneath her ear.

"You are the most daring, exciting, sensual woman I've ever met," he whispered.

Dora went still, waited for more. For words of love.

Were these the words he used in place of love? The words that meant the same?

She leaned her upper body back, gave him free access to her breasts, felt chills ripple up and down her spine as his lips toyed with her, pleasured her, drove her wild.

"Ethan, now."

He positioned her over him, entered her and held utterly, erotically still. With his hands wrapped firmly around her hips, he was in control.

She tried to hurry him along.

"Wait, sweetheart." His voice was rough and low. "Give me a minute."

He'd never called her sweetheart before. And the way he said it made Dora dream. Maybe these were Ethan's love words, or as close as he could come. Perhaps they could be a family after all.

And neither one of them would have to give up Katie.

His fingers loosened on her hips and now he guided her into a gentle rhythm that soon became impatient.

He swore, buried his lips in her throat. "You make me crazy. I can't get enough."

"Then take all you want." And he did. With healing waters lapping, and hands, lips and bodies rushing and straining, he took. And although Dora gave, she also took. Everything Ethan had to give her.

Chapter Thirteen

Ethan stood around after church, waiting for the women to finish setting up the potluck luncheon. Amazingly enough, Dora had pulled a chilled gelatin salad out of the refrigerator that morning. He should have known she'd understand and remember church schedules and such.

He felt out of sorts—guilty if the truth be known—imagining that everyone knew he'd taken advantage of a preacher's daughter. Never mind that she'd made it impossible to resist, that she *kept* making it impossible for him to resist. She deserved better.

He watched the way she spoke with the ladies, and the men, for that matter. She touched and held court and moved among his friends as though she were a hostess at a party, making everyone feel welcome and special. She was a natural at it, and though the town should have been the ones to see to her welcome, it wasn't necessary. Dora just automatically seemed to belong.

When she laughed at something Dan Lucas said,

putting her hand on the pastor's shoulder, Ethan scowled.

"What's wrong, Callahan? You're so used to women falling at your feet you don't know what to do now that you've met one who's giving you a run for your money?"

"Shut up, Wyatt." He didn't need to ask to know that his friends had seen him watching Dora. He had to wonder if his tongue had been hanging out.

Unrepentant, Wyatt grinned at Ethan's surly tone. Stony merely raised a brow and leaned against the wall, keeping an eye on his daughter as Nikki frolicked with Ian. He was a giant of a man, soft spoken, but tough. He could gentle a horse like no one else, yet Ethan had seen him use his fists, too. Stony was one of those guys poets liked to wax on about still waters running deep.

Ethan drew in a breath, thought about apologizing for his moodiness, then dismissed the idea. He'd grown up with these guys. They wouldn't take it personally.

"I like your Dora," Wyatt said.

"She's not mine."

"Hmm. Eaten any oysters lately?"

Ethan frowned. "What are you talking about?"

Stony, too, was looking a little bewildered. Wyatt shrugged. "Never mind. Just something Hannah mentioned."

Ethan had no idea what Hannah and oysters had to do with him, but he didn't have the energy to get into it. Wyatt was deliriously happy with his new wife and family. And though Ethan was happy for his friend, he'd begun to feel a distance growing between them. It was strictly on his part, he knew. But Wyatt now had a family, and Stony had Nikki.

And Ethan was odd man out. Alone.

Just as he wanted. Just as he'd always been happy with, he reminded himself.

"Oysters are supposed to be aphrodisiacs," Wyatt commented, evidently deciding to enlighten them, after all. "And olives, according to Hannah."

"Olives…" Ethan frowned. An image of Dora watching him intently as he ate green olives on their picnic flashed in his mind.

Wyatt nodded, and Stony was looking highly interested, although he was as much in the dark about the direction of the conversation as Ethan was.

"Seems Dora felt you needed a little help in the sex department."

"Help in…?" He frowned. "I do not."

Stony chuckled.

"Glad to hear it," Wyatt said.

"Are you telling me Dora discussed our sex life with your wife?"

"So there is a sex life?" Wyatt asked cagily.

"None of your business."

"There you go," Stony murmured, his nod clearly stating that Ethan's surly reply was an admission.

Wyatt just grinned.

Ethan was frustrated. "I'm not standing around in church discussing this subject. Do you guys want to eat or not?" Without waiting for an answer, he strode toward the food table.

He might have made it, too, but Dora flitted right

across the room and intercepted him, putting her hand on his arm and smiling up at him as though he'd gathered the sun and moon in his hands just for her. She held Katie in her arms and the baby reached out to grab a fistful of his shirt, effectively creating a connected circle of the three of them—as though they were a unit.

Why did that make his heart ache?

He glanced over her head and noticed his friends' telling smiles. Worse still were the four matchmakers standing off in a corner, watching and beaming.

Didn't these people know that a sinner and a saint didn't mix?

DORA CAREFULLY STACKED her sketches in her portfolio, pleased with the work she'd done. In the month she'd been at Ethan's ranch, she'd had plenty of inspiration. Her agent would be happy.

But time was ticking by. She had to get back to her work, her life. She had family obligations that she'd managed to cover, but only for the month. And according to the calendar, tomorrow would be thirty days.

She drew in a shaky breath, trying not to think about it.

Tidying up her work space—the only place where Dora truly paid attention to organization—her hand paused over a shelf of photographs. She picked them up, smiling at the photo of the tabby kitten peeking out of Ethan's hat. She remembered that morning, his incredulity that she would even dream of using his hat to hold an animal. She laughed when she flipped to the next picture of the golden-haired, baby Lab hanging over the lip of Ethan's boot.

In her hands was a visual journal of her month with the Callahans: Katie standing on the changing table, looking at Ethan as if he was her hero, her hand clutching his bandanna, Ethan's face lit with laughter and love; Ethan asleep on the couch with Katie sleeping on his chest; Ethan filthy after working with the horses; Ethan making googlie eyes at his baby daughter; Ethan with water dripping down his bare chest after a bout with a broken water pipe.

Oh, he was so incredibly handsome. She ought to submit these photos as a calendar proposal. It would sell like mad.

Her throat closed and her eyes filled with tears as she turned to the last photograph. It was one of her holding Katie in her arms.

She had to make a decision. But how could she? How could she give up Katie? That precious baby girl she'd loved like her own since Katie had drawn her first breath.

How could she ask Ethan to give her up?

They should have talked about this, somehow introduced the subject of visitation in the eventuality that her heart's desire wouldn't come to pass. It wasn't like her to bury her head in the sand, but that's exactly what she'd been doing all these weeks.

She had to face some real truths. She couldn't stay here forever—well, maybe she could, but that would compromise everything she believed in, who she was. She hadn't gotten Ethan to fall in love with her yet, and if she hadn't accomplished that goal in a month, was she kidding herself to think that she'd eventually have success if she just stayed a little longer?

He'd made it clear from the beginning that he wouldn't offer marriage. To any woman.

And Dora couldn't continue to live with him, outside the bonds of matrimony.

She knew the problem wouldn't go away by ignoring it, but that's exactly what she tried to do— *again*—as she grabbed her sketch pad and pencils and went in search of Ethan and Katie. Moments were precious now, and she couldn't afford to waste them. She needed to take every opportunity to spend every possible minute with the child she loved so. And the man. Just in case.

A patch of dandelions grew like a miniature meadow at the corner of the lawn. She picked a bunch and spent several minutes weaving the stems into a circlet. It was a purely fanciful endeavor, as they would wilt in a matter of an hour, but the crown of yellow weeds appealed to her.

Stopping by the stall where Katie's baby horse trotted friskily around, Dora clicked her tongue and reached her hand over the chest-high door.

"Come here, sweet baby." Without a shy bone in its body, the little filly trotted over, its mother close behind, eyeing Dora as though checking her out to see if she was worthy and safe enough to trust with her offspring.

As the foal nuzzled Dora's hand, she impulsively laid the circlet of dandelions over its ears and grinned at the absolutely darling pose.

"Be still for just a minute." She whipped out her

sketch pad and furiously began to sketch, smiling as she drew little pointy ears, a little tuft of mane sticking up between them, a wreath of simple flowers dipping low over the baby horse's inquisitive, velvety brown eyes.

Ethan came to a halt just outside of the tack room, his heart jolting when he saw Dora sketching like mad. He couldn't stop the smile that formed when he saw the crown of flowers on the foal's head. The woman just flat-out charmed him.

"Look what she's done to your horsey," he said softly to Katie. She clapped her hands and wiggled to get down. Ethan checked for obstacles. The concrete floors were clean enough to eat off, and Katie was wearing little bitty tennis shoes. Shouldn't hurt, he thought.

He set Katie down on her feet and steadied her with his palms. She was such an independent little cuss, she didn't want him to hold tight.

"You're going to fall," he cautioned, but he released his hold, allowing her to grip just his two forefingers.

When he glanced up, Dora had stopped sketching and was watching them, smiling. She squatted down and held out her hands, and just that simply, Katie released Ethan's fingers and took an unsteady step, then another.

Ethan was so stunned and excited he hovered right behind her, hardly daring to breathe, his hands out and ready to catch her if she fell. He wanted to shout and have everyone come running, to witness this amazing feat his daughter had accomplished. But he didn't want to startle her.

Dora was half-kneeling, stretching closer. Katie shrieked in pure glee and toddled right into her waiting arms.

"You smart girl! You walked." She lifted the baby and buried her lips in Katie's pudgy cheeks.

Ethan was right there, his arms around both of them, adding his own kisses to his daughter.

"Did you see that?" he asked rhetorically, beaming with pride. "She walked."

Dora muffled a laugh. "She sure did. Want to try it again?"

"So soon?" Surely her little legs were tired. It had been touch-and-go there for a minute. She'd looked a lot like a spindly legged foal trying to find its balance.

"Of course. Move back." She set Katie down and steadied her. "Go to Daddy," she whispered.

Ethan was several feet away, his arms outstretched, emotions crowding his chest. *Go to Daddy.* The title still caught him by surprise, awed him.

With his intent gaze still on Katie, the angry strike of hooves against concrete and the scuffle of boots drew his attention. Danger raised the hair on his nape a millisecond before he identified the source. Before he could blink or react, the joyous experience of his daughter's first steps turned into a nightmare right before his eyes.

A new stallion that Manny was leading into the stable reared out of control, striking at the stalls and everyone in his path. Ethan should have known better than to be playing in here. This was a working stable filled with spirited, expensive, unpredictable horses. No place to set a baby on the ground.

Men shouted and groped for lead ropes, trying to hold the stallion back, settle him. Nostrils flaring, hooves striking, he broke free and charged toward Dora and Katie.

Grant and Clay shouted. For an instant Dora froze, Katie cradled in her arms. Her back was against the wall, and she had nowhere to go. She turned and curled into herself, huddled there, covering Katie, leaving herself exposed.

Ethan threw himself into the stallion's path, waving his arms wildly. With a horribly surreal feeling, as though his legs were hardly moving, as though his entire body was sluggish, just like in the nightmares he sometimes had, he tried to reach Dora and Katie. At the last instant, he hurled himself against her back, pressing her solidly against the wall of the stable, shielding them with his own body.

The stallions hind quarters rammed into him, slamming him harder against Dora. Muscles strained as he tried to form a barricade around them with his arms, his hands planted against the wall, but his strength was no match against the mighty shove of the spooked animal and he couldn't help but smash Dora and Katie against the unyielding wall.

Katie screamed as though she'd been mortally wounded. He was afraid to look.

Despite Grant's and Clay's efforts to subdue the stallion, he broke away from the lead ropes and stampeded through the open end of the stable.

"Is everyone all right?" Grant called, his voice full of fear and concern.

Ethan couldn't answer for a minute. His mouth was bone-dry and his heart was ramming brutally against his rib cage.

He turned Dora and Katie in his arms. "Are you okay?" Katie still cried as though the world had ended, her mouth wide open, nose running, big tears drenching her face. "The baby?" He ran his hands over both Katie and Dora, checking for scrapes on their faces.

"We're fine," Dora said, her voice trembling.

"But Katie. Why's she crying so hard?"

"She's just scared."

Katie reached for Ethan, and he took her into his arms. Grant and Clay were still hovering.

"Everyone's fine," Ethan said, not feeling fine at all. His insides were quaking and his knees felt like water. He wanted to sit. "Make a note of that stallion's temperament. We'll want to think twice before we use his sperm."

"Cat ran under his feet," Clay said. "Wasn't really his fault."

"Watch him in any case. Better yet, get Stony over here to work with him, give an opinion."

"Good idea," Grant said. "I'll take care of it. Sure you're all right, Dora?"

"I'm fine."

Katie had stopped crying, but was still snuffling. With her head on Ethan's shoulder and a wad of his shirt clutched in her fist, she was gazing out at everyone as though they'd deliberately upset her but her daddy was going to make it right.

Dora felt a stinging in her stomach, and her heart. Like a knife slicing through delicate flesh, it had wounded her when Katie had reached for Ethan. It shouldn't have, and she felt small for feeling this way. She loved Ethan. And Ethan loved Katie. She truly wanted them to be a family.

Still, Katie had been hers for much longer than she'd been Ethan's. She'd always relied on Dora to protect her, had always wanted Dora to soothe her when life threw her a curve.

Her heart started pounding harder. *Stop it, Dora. Don't borrow trouble before it finds you.*

But she knew. Trouble had indeed found her.

Ethan turned back to her, studied her, reached out to tenderly brush her forehead. "You'll probably have a bruise, but the skin's not broken."

Dora examined the spot with her own fingers. "I didn't even notice."

"Does it hurt?" he asked softly, still watching her in an odd manner.

His gentleness made her want to weep. Dora shook her head, studied him, her gaze clinging, asking silent questions. They'd had a scare. Emotions were running high. This was the perfect opportunity for him to declare his feelings.

Yet, instead of declarations, he stepped back, both emotionally and physically.

And suddenly Dora knew exactly what that look had meant.

He cared, as anyone would who'd been intimate

with another person. But he still couldn't, *wouldn't* make promises. A commitment.

Wanting to scream, she swallowed hard and cupped his cheek. Her smile was sad, an apology, a gesture of reluctant understanding. A wish that things could be different.

Time's up, she thought, knowing her heart was in her eyes, but helpless to do anything about it.

"Ask me to stay," she whispered.

He looked as though she'd struck him. "I can't. I'm no good for you, Dora."

"Shouldn't I be the judge of that?"

He shook his head. "You deserve someone much better than me."

She could have hit him. But he was safe at the moment since he held the baby. She took a deep breath, tried to control her frustration.

"If you don't think you're good enough for me, what about Katie?"

"That's different. She's my blood. She doesn't have a choice. But you do, legs. You can have someone better."

Her fist was seriously itching to take a swing. She ignored the latter part of his statement and concentrated on the first. "Katie has a choice. Adoption."

"Never." His voice was resolute.

And Dora realized it was hopeless. She had to admit that Ethan was an excellent father. He loved his little girl. And Katie loved him. There was no way he'd give her up. And besides that, he had a legal right to the child. He was Katie's father.

Dora was only a friend.

"I have a confession to make," she began softly. "I didn't just come here to fulfill my promise to Amanda. I came to persuade you to give Katie to me. I thought you'd realize that a baby didn't fit in with your lifestyle and it would be a piece of cake to get you to sign over adoption papers."

"You never mentioned—"

She shook her head, interrupted. "No. Because I changed my mind. Because I was greedy. I decided I wanted it all."

"All?"

"Katie *and* you."

He stared at her in utter confusion, as though she'd taken him totally by surprise, as if the possibility that she might have deeper feelings for him had never occurred to him.

That was the final nail in her coffin.

She hesitated one last moment, waited…for a lightning bolt, an admission of undying love, she didn't know what. His hat shaded his eyes, but she still saw the compassionate look. Dear Lord, it was pity.

Well, she'd truly made a fool of herself. But she could remedy that. She could pretend a sophistication she didn't in any way feel.

Giving him a gentle smile, a smile intended to release him of any guilt or obligations, she turned and walked away.

WITHIN AN HOUR of the near tragedy in the barn, Ethan was a mess. Katie sensed something was wrong and she was fussing. Nothing he did for her would settle her. Grant and Clay had even given it a turn, but to no avail.

Feeling his gut twist in panic, he watched as Dora came down the stairs carrying two suitcases and a huge duffel bag.

All the belongings she'd brought with her.

Only hers, though. Not Katie's.

Her shoulders were square, but her beautiful face was raw with sadness.

"Are you sure?" he asked, his own throat aching.

"It's time."

"But Katie just learned to walk. There's still toilet training to go through."

Dora smiled and made an effort not to look at Katie. She wouldn't be able to hold in the horrendously clawing emotions if she looked. If she touched.

"You'll manage just fine."

"But she'll miss you," he argued.

"Babies are resilient." She swallowed hard, willed her voice not to break. "She'll forget about me soon enough and bounce back." Just the idea of being forgotten by this precious baby tore Dora in two.

In his own way Ethan was asking her to stay. But for Katie. Not for him.

She needed a much stronger reason than the baby's welfare. She needed to be asked to stay for love.

And for marriage.

That's just who she was.

She had to leave before she totally lost it. There was nothing worse than messy goodbyes.

He wasn't going to stop her. She realized that now. Actually, she'd realized that from the beginning, even though she'd held on to a fragile hope. She'd gone into the intimacy with her eyes wide open. She couldn't cry foul. And she wouldn't.

"Katie loves you, Ethan. And you love her. You're going to be a great father."

Chapter Fourteen

Katie's wail escalated to a piercing scream when Dora walked out the door.

"Shh, baby, shh." He didn't know what to do. He'd just let Dora slip through his fingers. But damn it, he didn't have a right to stop her.

"Great going, bro," Grant said above Katie's heartbroken cries. Both Grant and Clay had been unashamedly eavesdropping from the kitchen. "Are you just going to let her walk out?"

"What else can I do?"

"Stop her."

"I can't."

"Give me that baby," Clay said with a look of disgust for Ethan's incredible stupidity. "There, now, doll baby. Come tell Uncle Clay all about it." He shook his head. "Uncle Grant will tell your daddy what a big idiot he is."

Ethan's emotions were in excruciating turmoil as it was. He didn't need this kind of abuse from his brothers, too.

His fists clenched at his sides. Katie was still crying, even though Clay had taken her into the kitchen and was doing his best to soothe. It wasn't right. That baby shouldn't be so heartbroken. It was his job to see to it.

"I didn't protect them today," he said to Grant. "In the stable."

He nodded. "They could've been seriously injured. Killed. What if it happens again and I'm not around? What if I *can't* protect them?" He'd sworn he would never feel that kind of responsibility again.

And trust Grant to know exactly what Ethan was dancing around, the underlying truth beneath his questions.

"You've got to let that go, Ethan. We're not kids anymore and we're not in Chicago. That part of our life is over."

"Is it? Don't you still have nightmares about that slimeball our mother brought home? That miserable excuse for a human who tried to put his hands on you?"

Grant winced. "That had nothing to do with you."

"The hell it didn't. I was the oldest. It was my responsibility. You guys were my responsibility."

"No. We were our mother's."

Ethan felt his insides twist. He was grabbing at straws and he knew it. Katie was still crying so hard he wondered if she'd make herself sick.

"What if I'm like her?" He didn't even want to think it. But here was the root of his character, the reason he lived his life the way he did, felt the way he did.

"Like who?"

"Our mother. She couldn't commit to a long-term relationship. She went from man to man. You know as well as I do that we all have different sperm donors, and there's not a whole hell of a lot of age difference between us." He rarely thought about the fact that they each had a biological father out there somewhere.

"What if there's some renegade gene embedded in me despite the decent upbringing Dad gave us? What if it breaks through and turns me into the kind of man who'd feel trapped waking up to the same woman every day."

"It's not like you to say stupid things, Ethan." Grant ignored the flare of anger in Ethan's face. "Can you honestly imagine feeling that way about Dora?"

"Not right now. I hardly get anything done because I just want to stand around and take a good long while looking at that face. But what about later?"

"You can't live your life based on what-ifs. What if later never comes? What if the nasty gene's not there? Do you want to spend the rest of your life waiting for the boogeyman to jump out at you?"

"Get real."

"No, you get real." Grant's tone held a snap to it now. "Genetics aside, Ethan, you have a choice. You've seen Stony make champions out of horses who through no fault of their own have inherited bad traits. They become champions because they have heart. And that's stronger than a renegade gene."

Ethan began to hope. And to realize that he'd really screwed up. He *did* want to wake up to Dora's face every day, her disorganization, her sass and her innocence and her verve. She was a woman who would never bore him. A forever kind of woman. "I'm a fool."

"You won't get any argument here. Do you love her?"

Five minutes ago he would have been stunned by the immediate answer that sprang to his lips.

"Yes." He tested the affirmation, felt his heart kick up a beat. "Yes. Absolutely."

"Did you tell her?"

He shook his head. "Why would I? I didn't even know till just now." It simply hadn't occurred to him to examine his feelings and recognize them for what they were. He'd been a playboy bachelor for so long, the proper way of doing things was foreign to him.

He didn't think he'd ever said, *I love you* to any woman except his mom—and she'd dumped him off on strangers.

And since then he'd never met anyone he wanted to spend more than a few weeks with. He was rich and spoiled, he realized. Before, he could always hop in the plane and fly off somewhere if he got bored. His money meant he could play and have anybody and anything he wanted.

"Then I guess you didn't have enough sense to ask her to stay? Offer her marriage? Because with a woman like Dora, you can't offer anything less. You hurt her, Ethan. That look on her face as she walked out nearly tore my heart out. She's the best thing that's happened to any of us, and if you don't recognize that—"

"See if you can give Clay a hand with Katie," he

interrupted and charged out of the house, his heart pounding. He might not have been able to find the wherewithal to stop her from walking out the door, but he could darned well catch her, convince her to stay. Beg if need be.

He only had one burning goal as he ripped open the door and ran outside. He'd never anticipated tripping over a pile of suitcases strewn on the porch. As he tumbled down the porch steps, his mind grabbed on to a single image.

Dora.

Sitting on the porch steps, her head on her knees, her arms over her head, hands covering her ears.

He picked himself up off the ground, wanted to shout with joy. It was just like his Dora to leave things strewn about, creating tripping hazards.

Instead, he just stood there, his chest swelling with emotion, his throat aching with it. Their eyes met and held. Hers were red rimmed and her cheeks were wet with tears.

He ought to be strung up by his toes for hurting her this way. For being such an idiot.

"I thought you left," he said softly.

"I did." She sniffed, and her voice hitched.

"But you're still here," he pointed out.

"My feet wouldn't go any farther."

His brows lifted. "How come?"

"They have this thing about going someplace if everything else in me doesn't go along with them."

"Your *feet* object?" He was a little confused, but that was nothing new around Dora. And she had such a charming way of confusing him.

"Yes."

"What wasn't going with them?"

"My heart. I left it here."

Ah. He felt more confident now. "I suppose you expect me to give it back. Your heart, that is."

She glared at him with hurt and accusation. "You already gave it back when you let me walk out the door."

"I ought to be shot," he said, but she obviously wasn't paying attention.

"I know it's pitiful, but I can't help it. It doesn't seem to matter that you don't want my heart or my love."

"But I do."

She shook her head, stared at the toes of her sneakers. "I heard Katie crying. You just need somebody to care for her."

"No. I need *you*."

Dora jerked her head up, looked at him closely. Something in his tone made butterflies flutter in her stomach. But she was so afraid to hope.

"You're the mother of my child."

If only that were so. She would give anything to have carried that baby in her womb, to ensure that no one could ever take her little girl away. She started to shake her head.

He reached for her then, cupped her elbows, drew her to her feet. "Yes. You are Katie's mother in every way that counts."

Oh. His words were the most wonderful gift he could have given her.

"I love you," he said softly, then took a deep

breath. "That was a tough one. I didn't think I'd ever say those words to a woman. To anyone. Now I just want to say it again."

Dora's heart was bursting. She had all she wanted. All she needed right here. Almost. "Feel free to keep right on."

"I love you." He touched his lips to hers. "Please stay."

Ethan watched the light of mirth flash in her lake-blue eyes and braced himself. Here he was, in the most serious moment of his life, and she had merriment written all over her.

"My daddy, being a preacher and all, doesn't normally go in for violence, but he might think about oiling up the twelve-gauge if I keep hanging around here living with a bunch of playboy bachelor cowboys."

Now that kind of talk terrified Ethan. Shotguns, that was. Not, surprisingly enough, the thought of marriage. Yes, on the subject of marriage he was at peace and suddenly in a very big hurry.

"Do you love me, legs?"

"Of course."

He grinned. Man he was crazy about her. "Then I guess you ought to make an honest man out of me."

"An honest…?" She burst out laughing and threw her arms around his neck, easing right up against his body in a way that made him hard in an instant and thankful he was alive.

"Yeah. You're gonna have to marry me, legs."

"Mmm. It's a tough job, but somebody's got to do it."

"You're all heart."

"Yes. I am. And all my heart belongs to you and Katie. I love you, Ethan Callahan."

As she took his lips and soul-kissed him right down to his toes, Ethan had one last thought.

Ozzie and the rest of the fellas had known exactly what they were doing. And the way he felt about Dora, not only would Shotgun Ridge's population increase by another woman and a baby, there was sure to be plenty more babies to follow—not to mention the menagerie of animals Dora Watkins Callahan would drag onto his ranch and into his heart.

With the phone cord wrapped around her finger, Eden Williams turned and nearly fainted.

Stony Stratton was standing behind her, unashamedly listening to her telephone conversation.

Her heart surged so hard she actually saw stars.

"I've got to go, Aunt Lottie," she whispered. Like an inferno, the heat of chagrin drenched her. "Talk to you soon." Eden hung up the phone, rubbed her damp palms on the seat of her jeans and turned to face the music. Or Stony, rather.

"So, has Lottie recovered from her stress?"

Eden nodded. His gaze was fixed so steadily on her it took every bit of her will not to squirm.

"Thought so." He took off his hat, bounced it gently against his thigh. Although his voice was achingly pleasant, he was clearly annoyed. "Don't you think it's time you told me what's really going on? Why you're here?"

Think, Eden. Don't blow it. She opened her mouth, felt her heart nearly pound out of her chest.

"I need to have a baby." Adrenaline shot through

her so fast she had to grab the countertop for support. It felt as though her lungs had collapsed, and try as she might, she couldn't seem to draw in enough air to chase away the dizziness.

She'd told Aunt Lottie she couldn't just blurt it out, yet that's exactly what she'd done.

And there was no turning back now.

When he didn't react, didn't move so much as an eyelash, she tried again, her voice and hands trembling with fear and embarrassment…and a quiet desperation that squared her shoulders and lifted her chin, gave her courage.

"I want you to get me pregnant."

In the silence that followed they could have heard an ant sneeze.

Stony blinked, stared, then jammed his hat on his head, and without a single word or change in expression, he turned and walked out the door.

MAITLAND MATERNITY

Where the luckiest babies are born!

Join Harlequin® and Silhouette® for a special 12-book series about the world-renowned Maitland Maternity Clinic, owned and operated by the prominent Maitland family of Austin, Texas, where romances are born, secrets are revealed…and bundles of joy are delivered!

Look for

MAITLAND MATERNITY

titles at your favorite retail outlet, starting in August 2000

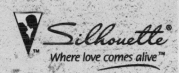

COMING NEXT MONTH

Visit us at www.eHarlequin.com

CNM0700